MW01490889

Sweet Lies and Silent Vows

A. C. Winter

Content Warning

This book contains graphic scenes of violence, strong language and explicit descriptions of sex. Reader discretion is advanced if you find any of the following triggering.

Triggers include:
Anal sex, Attempt of sexual assault, Blood, Bullying, Car accident, Child abuse (backstory), Chocking, Desecration of a corpse, Drowning, Doxxing, Execution, Foot play, Gun play, Mental illness, Murder, Orgasm denial, Rape, Sexual harassment, Spanking, Suicide, Trauma.

Dedication:

To that one friend who lured me to the dark side.

Authors note:

This book is a work of fiction. The people, places or events in this book are not real nor do I claim any ethnicity, religious group or organization to have anything to do with the contents of this story.

This whole process began from a writing challenge that turned into a complete book. During the writing process I used a lot of real life experiences depicting real emotions for the characters, making them feel more real and come to life. At least for myself. This whole journey has challenged me as a writer and encouraged me to reach out of my comfort zone and become an actual author. I did not think Sweet lies and silent vows would be my debut, though, but I look forward to publishing more stories I have up my sleeve.

That being said, I hope you enjoy this book about a brave but mistreated woman, who ends up being used as a puppet by the patriarchy and how she fought against it. This is her story.

"I dare you not to sing Little lies by Fleetwood Mac while reading Sweet lies and silent vows by A.C. Winter." — In regards, author.

Chapter 1

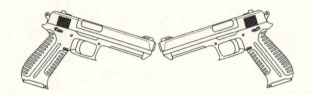

Did you know, once a year, the wealthiest leaders of the underground network gathered together at a venue with their associates and laid down their arms? At least once a year the city slept soundly, unknowingly that the ruthless, most dangerous gangsters, drug lords and criminals were band together to celebrate Christmas. Today was one of those rare occasions.

I had spent most of the evening taking turns dancing under the chandeliers with whomever happened to step in front of me. Due to downing a sparkling wine flute between songs, I lost track of them hours ago. Logan was far too eager to have me all to himself on the dance floor, but thanks to my cousin Erica, I managed to slip away unnoticed. Despite his many attempts to win me over for years, I wasn't interested in him. Or in any other guy for that matter.

Being the direct descendants of the most influential crime lord of the city had its risks. More often than not, the loved ones were the first to suffer. Just like my mother, just like so many others before her had been used as a pawn and paid the price, and I was not ready to join them. Instead, I enjoyed what little freedom I still had before my time was up.

My eyes wandered around the glamorous ballroom from the festive garlands to the massive pine tree in the corner decorated with hundreds of glass baubles, velvet ribbons, and bells.

Securing another glass in my hand and successfully avoiding another dance with Logan, I slipped behind the band and shimmied my way to the balcony. The city was never quiet even on a silent night such as this. Somewhere below I heard the siren of a fire truck howling. As I stayed in the cold, I formed vapors in the air which felt wonderful against my heated cheeks.

Eventually I was forced to meander back inside in search of the bathroom. A tall figure stood near the door, completely taken by the shadows, only the glow of their cigarette illuminating their features. He was dressed in a well tailored suit, a black shirt and shiny leather shoes. I would have to walk past him to get back to the ballroom.

"Excuse me." I said, clearing my throat as I shuffled through the archway in attempts to avoid touching him. He made no movements to let me pass and continued to stare at me along their nose. *Prick.*

"You are excused." He exhaled a puff of smoke. Something in his voice had all the hair in the back of my neck standing up. When I looked back, I could have sworn his eyes were glowing red. Or maybe it was the wine playing tricks on me. I quickly gathered my composure and tossed my hair back.

"Did you know you are standing under a mistletoe?" I nodded to the small green bundle hanging from the ceiling right above the archway.

"Are you expecting a kiss?"

My eyes fell on his lips. *Hell yes.* I made the assumption he would be a great kisser, but he acted as if that was the last thing on his mind.

"No." A white lie. I wouldn't mind being kissed by a tall, mysterious and handsome man in the dark, but I wasn't going to admit that to his face. "Just a friendly warning."

"We're not friends." He muttered, taking another inhale of his cigarette and blowing out the smoke.

"Then perhaps you are the one waiting for a kiss." Was I flirting with him? Maybe the last glass of wine was too much, I thought to myself. I was feeling bold, leaning on the door frame, licking my lip seductively. I was dying to taste him.

"You shouldn't wander alone." He leaned in, stealing my breath as he stared menacingly into my eyes. *Damn, he's handsome.* He had that old school charm about him, just like they did in the old black and white movies. His sharp jaw complimented his straight nose and high cheekbones, carved to perfection.

"I'm not alone, am I?" *Seriously, I've got to stop. No more sparkling wine for me tonight.* My voice was ridiculously breathy, I hardly recognized myself. He stood so close to me I could feel the heat radiating off his body.

"You keep dangerous company." He placed one hand on the granite wall behind my head, flashing the empty holster for his gun. It was big, making me wonder what else was big about him. The other hand traced the contour of my side, making me sway, chasing his touch. *This is a bad idea.*

"I like danger. Isn't that what we do? Play with danger every day?"

"I don't play." His hands weaved into my hair, tugging at the roots, making my back bend for him. He pressed me up against the wall and caged my body entirely as his teeth grazed my neck. The deep rumble against my sensitive skin was my undoing. "I control it."

His lips fell on mine and I was unable to withhold the moan as he sucked on my bottom lip. Our tongues danced and breaths mingled in a wild collision of our desire to devour one another. He tasted like cigarettes and whiskey, and the way his hands roamed along my body set my insides ablaze.

Far too soon, I heard approaching footsteps coming towards our direction. I recognized the voices of my father's guards. They were looking for me. *Shit*. The man above me went rigid as he too had heard the intruding notion. He pulled me further into the shadows, and then we waited for them to pass while holding our breaths. He was so close I could kiss him again by a slight tilt of my head.

"This was a mistake." He whispered, when they had gone, and took a few steps back, making distance between us. The air felt cold once more and it was a slap of reality. It had been a mistake. A wonderful, sexy mistake. He raked the gel in his hair, smoothing over what I had destroyed, returning his appearance to the flawless statue.

Missing his touch, I groaned. It had been the most intense feeling I had experienced in my entire life. I wasn't a virgin for a long shot and had had my fair share of one night stands, but none of them held a candle to what had just transpired between us. Reeling back some of my composure, I finally managed to tear my eyes away from him.

"Yeah, I agree. This can't happen again." No matter how much I wanted it.

Seeing my own reflection in the window, I appeared every bit disheveled. My makeup was smeared, a few ringlets had fallen out of place and my dress had hiked up my thighs. I looked like I had just been hit by a sex tornado and I couldn't stop smiling at the culprit. Our eyes met, and before I even had a chance to straighten up my appearance, his mouth was all over me again, branding me.

"Never again." He murmured, nibbling at my jaw.

"Never." I kissed him long and hard one last time, and then he was gone. His scent lingered on my skin and the feel of his body was still fresh on my fingertips. How I craved to be touched by him again.

But that's all it was, a craving, a moment of lust. I would never allow myself to get attached. I entertained the idea of commitment long enough to feel a warm body laying on top of before never seeing them again. It was for the best. No loved one meant no one to hurt, no one to lose and no one to miss when they were gone. It was better that way, I thought, leaving the bitter cold that followed me in my heart.

After another round at the bar, I spotted my cousin, who was frantically trying to get my attention across the room.

"Where the hell have you been?" Erica hissed, grabbing me by the elbow just as I swallowed a crabcake; my favorite of the hors d'oeuvres. "Your father is furious. He was gonna send the dogs after you."

"I was just in the bathroom. What's gotten his panties in a twist?"

"I don't know, but he told me to find you asap."

"One night. Couldn't he relax for one night just like the rest of us?"

"I wish. He is upstairs. Go." She gently guided me towards the stairs. I began the intimidating ascent, one hand on to the railing and my other hand holding on to the hem of my dress. Looking down I saw Erica still following my steps with her eyes. She gave me a wink, tossed her black hair over her shoulder and mouthed silently. "And find me when you're done. I just saw the Laurenzo boys enter the ballroom."

She was a hopeless romantic. Almost the polar opposite of myself. Where she dreamed of a big wedding, a doting husband and a handful of chubby babies, I just wanted to live alone, in some house with a back yard, away from the city and this dreadful life.

Below me was the glimmering ballroom, filled with people dressed to the nines and to my right large oaken doors leading to the private lounge. I corrected my lipstick, straightened the wrinkles out of my dress and raked my hair once over before stepping towards the door. The two goons standing at guard nodded and ushered me in.

My father was sitting in a leather chair close to a fireplace, turning the ice in his glass. Another man sat opposite of him, his back to the door. A handful of men stood guard by the windows and doors. The atmosphere seemed charged even though the room was set up with cozyness in mind. Striding across the carpet, I leaned down to greet my father before settling beside him.

"You summoned me, Papa?"

"Valentina, do you remember Mr. O'Hara?" He said with feigned enthusiasm, gesturing to the man who stood up and offered their hand to greet me. He had a prominent mustache and a receding hairline, and when he smiled, wrinkles gathered in the corners of his eyes.

"Ah yes of course. Mr. O'Hara, glad you could make it this year. It's so good to see you again." *I have no memory of when I last saw this man. Am I supposed to? Why does that name ring a bell?* I keep up with my perfect smile but give my father 'the eyes' screaming 'help me'.

"Pleasure is all mine, angel."

He sat back down, taking a long swing out of his glass and measuring me up and down with his eyes. I suppressed a shiver when he lingered on my breasts for far too long to be appropriate. *Ew.*

"Yes, she will do." He hummed, satisfied with me apparently and waved one of his ringed fingers. He whispered something to one of his goons who saluted and left without saying a word.

"What is this about?"

"Ah, well, you see, Mathias and I have some special business together. Very special."

"It's Christmas, Papa. Can't that wait?"

"What better time to seal the deal when all the participants are under the same roof and properly softened with drinks and good company, eh?"

"If you say so, but what does this have to do with me? Why am I here?" I had an odd feeling in my gut and it had nothing to do with the alcohol I had consumed earlier.

"Malyshka, you will serve as insurance till the deal has come through."

"Insurance? What do you mean 'insurance'?"

"We have decided you will be married off to-"

"Married?!"

"The wedding will be held before the New Years, nothing fancy, just a formality really. You will have to move in with him of course. And if there should be children, well, that's your problem then. Don't expect the boy to pay any child support. It will all be in the contract."

"Wait wait wait, wait just a damn minute. Marriage? Children? Contract? Absolutely not."

"Malyshka! You're being rude to our guest."

"Papa, you can't be serious. I can't get married."

"You can and you will. End of."

"She has a temper. Jax will like that." My eyes flew to Mr. O'Hara who placed one leg over his knee, leaned back and put on a sleazy smile. *Who the hell is Jax?* I couldn't recall for the life of me anyone named Jax from all of my father's associates. "Think of it this way. It's only temporary. Give it a year, maybe two. As long as the deal doesn't fall through, you are free to go and carry on with your life."

"And if it does?" Both of them exchanged looks. They acted like bestest of chums, but under the fake smiles and pleasant conversation lay the hearts of venomous snakes. I could guess the consequence was a life in servitude or death.

The walls in the room began to fold in. I couldn't believe what they were suggesting. No, not suggesting. They had already decided my fate. Should the business go bust, I was to remain with the O'Hara's and they would be entitled to do whatever they pleased with me. A shiver ran along my spine and I swallowed the whimper that threatened to escape me. They could have me work till I was raw, or dead, it was all the same.

Or I could be stuck being married to someone I didn't even know. Hell, just being married was punishment enough. I had witnessed first hand what it was to be married to one of our kind. The countless times my mother begged for mercy that never came and one time it was too much, she couldn't take it anymore and she took her own life. That was the fate of a mafia wife.

I tried to steady my breath but there was no air left in the room. I was suffocating under the pressure of their eyes on me. I realized there was no escape if they had their way. No matter what they chose, I would be doomed either way. I couldn't let that happen. Biting down to my last shred of fight left in me, I put my foot down and stood against my father.

"No. I'm sorry but the answer is no."

"Valentina!" There was a threatening rumble in his voice, but I was too stupid and ignored it.

"No! Please reconsider. There has to be another way."

He moved faster than I had ever seen him move. He lunged out of the chair, wrapped his hands around my neck and squeezed in tightly. My vision blurred and all I could see was his red face staring back at me. My nails dug into his arms in a desperate attempt to free myself from his grasp, but it only made him press on tighter on my windpipe.

"I'm done talking about this. My decision is final." He hissed in our native tongue.

"I-I won't go through with this. You c-can't make me." I choked out.

"Defy me again and I will show you just how easily I can make you. You don't make the rules here. I do. Now apologize to Mr. O'Hara and then I don't want to hear another sound out of you for the rest of the evening, are we clear?" When I didn't answer he rattled me in his hold till I caved and nodded. "Good."

He released me and with a heavy gasp I returned the air back into my lungs. His handprints were already throbbing and I bit my lip silencing the cry just thinking about the bruises that would form on my neck come morning. I bowed and gave a meek apology to our current company, keeping my head down even when I heard the oaken door open. Shined shoes appeared before me but I did not dare to look up.

"Ah, Jax, just in time. Come meet your new bride." There was a short pause before the man spoke. His voice was deep and mundane, like he was bored just being here.

"And what do you expect me to do with her, father?" *Father?*

"Keep her till I tell you otherwise, understand? Alive preferably."

"Fine." *Just fine? That's it, no fight?* If he only had disagreed with the older men I might have had a chance to plead my case again, but no. He accepted it, simple as that, like it meant nothing. Like I meant nothing. "And you agree to this?"

Another pause and I assumed he was asking me since I felt my father squeeze my arm more painful than was necessary. He was sending me a message. I nodded, like a damn fool, but it was the right response, because I felt my fathers fingers loosen their grip again.

"So it is settled. You two kids will make a lovely couple." Mr. O'Hara announced, clapping his hands together. "The ceremony will be held soon and I'll see that the papers are in order."

"Let us toast to the wonderful union of our families. Cheers." I heard the glasses clink and then the contents gulped down. I was not offered one and I wouldn't have taken it either. They were celebrating my funeral.

I kept my eyes to the ground, silently waiting for the whole thing to be over, until finally father grabbed me by the elbow and escorted me out, murmuring our farewells like I've had too much to drink for the night. Daring to look up after the car door slammed shut, I was only able to make out the silhouette of the man who would be my husband, and who held my life in his hands.

Chapter 2

The weather, like my emotions, was a blizzard. Standing in front of a mirror, I tugged at the long sleeves of my white gown to hide the bruises my father had given me as my something blue. Applying another layer of powder and blush, I hoped it would be enough to hide my black eye. Under it all I was broken.

Father had shown me exactly how I was to be treated when I didn't obey the man of the house the minute we got home that night. Every lash, every strike, every kick and punch he gave me was a reminder not to embarrass him in front of anyone ever again. To not disobey his orders. To not back talk, to not disagree, to do nothing but smile and nod.

Those were his words. I was to be the perfect little doll, submissive and quiet, for him and for all men. Especially my husband. He didn't hesitate to show me the kind of treatment that was waiting for me after the wedding if I even blinked the wrong way during the ceremony.

So I did what I thought was best for my survival. I

bit down, making a silent vow to pay back the hurt he had caused me. Burrowing my feelings deep under the surface, I pinned my veil up and put on a happy bride smile. The image in the mirror was not my own, but it was the one who stepped out of the bathroom and marched down the marriage bureau hallway. Every agonizing step echoed on the walls like a gunshot. I was a lamb to be slaughtered.

My father was ready by the door to walk me down the short aisle, smiling proudly. Ridiculous notion given the fact that he was the one who had brutally beaten me to the verge of death and I was no blushing bride. Either way, I took the small bundle of flowers, hooked my arm in his and faced the men waiting at the other end of the walk.

There were barely any witnesses to this farce. Mr. O'Hara with presumably his wife, my father's recent long term hook up, the officiant and only a few security details as always. My fiance stood next to the officiant, not even looking in my direction. *Good.* I didn't need him to see the reluctancy and the dread in my eyes. There was only so much I could hide.

"Dearly beloved-" The officiant began, but was immediately cut off by my father clearing his throat.

"Perhaps we can skip all the jibber jabber and get to the end. We are busy people after all. Let's speed the ceremony along, shall we?"

Stunned by my fathers audacity I made the error of looking back at him. His business-like smile faded slightly, giving me a silent threat to get back in line quickly lest I anger him again. I turned and with a passing glance noticed my fiance staring at me. *Shit.* It was too late to correct my mistake.

I faced the officiant, kept my eyes low, nodded and smiled, hoping it would be enough. *Maybe he will be merciful if I agree to the fast forward. Maybe, just maybe, if I play along he won't beat me as badly as my father did.* "Uh, shall I go on?" The officiant piped up, slightly shaken. I couldn't blame him, but I doubt he had any idea who was standing in front of him. He might as well be staring straight at death. I had to convince everyone, so I cleared my throat.

"Yes. Do as he says. Skip the speech, let's get to the vows."

"Alright then. Do you Jackal Blake O'Hara take Valentina Katerina Gregorovich as your lawfully wedded wife?"

"I do." Jackal said with that familiar mundane voice and placed a ring on my finger. A small rose gold band with a diamond and silver details. Delicate and beautiful. Exactly the kind of ring any bride would be happy to receive on their wedding day, apart from myself.

"And do you Valentina Katerina Gregorovich take Jackal Blake O'Hara as your lawfully wedded husband?"

"I do." My voice cracked. I could only hope the officiant would take it as wedding jitters. With trembling hands, I placed the band on Jackal's finger. Simple but elegant, featuring both silver and rose gold, a perfect match to mine. If only the match of our union was perfect too.

"By the powers invested in me I hereby declare you husband and wife. You may kiss the bride."

Fear boiled in my stomach. How could I have forgotten the kiss? I would have to kiss my husband and pretend like I was enjoying it, like I wanted it. Like I wanted any part in this sham of a marriage. I closed my eyes, hoping he would take the initiative and get it over with. Just a small peck. Quick and easy.

Instead, I felt warm hands, one by my hip, the other cradling my face. He pressed his lips on mine, softly, brushing over them ever so delicately with his tongue before taking over the pace of the kiss entirely. It was deep, sensual and consuming; and there was a strange familiarity to it. He tasted like cigarettes.

When we pulled away, the congratulations and other well wishes fell on deaf ears as I was utterly shocked at the view. It was him. *Him.* My midnight mystery man whom I'd kissed was staring back at me. Butterflies took flight, replacing the sensation in my stomach and sending shockwaves to my core.

The shock was followed by confusion. He pulled away, no hint of pleasure nor regret on his face, simply staring to the distance as if uninterested in the whole ordeal. *How could he keep a straight face in a moment like this? Doesn't he care at all? He must be in on the deal. Why else would he have agreed to the marriage so quickly? And why did he kiss me like that? Is that part of his ruse?*

The kiss had been every bit as fiery as the night we met. He would devour me if I'd let him. And even now when my body was still humming with pleasure, I was afraid my husband would be the death of me. I reminded myself to act carefully around him in the future.

"Right then. Now it's only the matter of signing the papers and you'll be off on your way." Mr. O'Hara gestured to the podium with our marriage license. Just some ink on a paper, our names signed on a single line, equal with the vows spoken.

But I knew, I just signed my name to the devil. Jackal O'Hara. The son of one of the most powerful crime lords, rumored to be the most ruthless man in the city even more so than his father. I never thought I'd put a face to the name, yet alone be married to him.

"Aww, look at them two." Mrs. O'Hara squealed, wiping her eyes. "You are going to enjoy the honeymoon." *I don't think so. I'll be sleeping with a knife under my pillow if he so much as shadows my doorstep.*

"That can wait. I have urgent business to attend to. I'll see to it that she is comfortable at my residence in my absence. Adieu."

Jackal fished a phone out of his pants pocket and proceeded to read through something simultaneously walking out of the office and down the corridor without looking back. I gave my father one last glance before bowing my head down and following my *husband.* My heels clacked on the marble floor as I rushed to catch up to him.

A car with tinted windows was waiting for us outside. He held the door for me as I climbed to the passenger seat, then proceeded to round the car to the driver side. He took his place as the pilot, switched the car in gear and drove us into the traffic.

The drive was silent, only the hum of the engine keeping us company. Jackal had his eyes pinned on the road. The deathgrip he had on the steering wheel was enough for me to know not to provoke him, so I let my gaze wander outside of the window. Multiple high risers framed the skyline and disappeared into the clouds. The streets were almost empty as only a few people dared the snow storm.

The car came to a slow stop in an underground garage. Jackal led me to an elevator and pressed the button to the penthouse. *Figures. Where else would a man like him live?*

"The house is empty for now." He said as he punched in

a key code. "My men are taking care of some things out of the country so you'll be on your own for a few days. I'm sure you'll manage."

"Yes, Mr. O'Hara." A voice not my own answered. I didn't want to sound too eager to know I'd have some time to adjust to my new surroundings without anyone breathing down my neck. Nervously I began to fidget with the ring on my finger.

"Jax." He said over his shoulder flicking on the lights of the apartment using a wall panel. "Call me Jax, or Jackal, whatever you prefer. You don't need to be so formal with me, wife."

"Katy." For the first time in an hour I finally looked into his eyes. They were a beautiful shade of brown and glowed in the dim light of the room. *I shouldn't stare but I can't help it. My husband is dangerously handsome.* "My first name is Valentina, but I like Katy. It's what my mother used to call me."

"Very well. There are three floors. First floor kitchen, common areas, living room, dining room etcetera." He waved his hand around pointing to different directions doing a full 360 turn on his heels. He seemed more relaxed now that we were at his home. "Second floor is for guests and the staff. I have five on call, including a housekeeper, Louisa. She doesn't speak a word of English but keeps the place spotless."

The place looked immaculate. Tall ceilings decorated with modern light features, white walls with massive paintings and the floors had beautiful tile patterns. Though I only got a small glimpse from my point of view, the furniture and the rest of the decor was very modern, elegant and expensive.

Walking up the stairs I could see the entire city spread

out through the floor to ceiling windows. The building reached so high we were almost swallowed up by the clouds. From the top floor I was barely able to hear the sounds of the city below.

"The third floor is for my personal use. Over there is my office, that is my bedroom." He said, pointing out each door and stopping in front of two large black doors. "And this is your room."

He waited for me to step in. The room was surprisingly feminine compared to the rest of the house. Taking a walk around the room I noticed the furniture was untouched and most likely new. The bed was freshly made with soft fabrics, armchair cushions were fluffed out and jewelry boxes were neatly organized by the vanity, ready to be filled.

"Bathroom is through there and I'll have your clothes brought to you by tomorrow. You can use whatever you like from my closet till then. That is, if you want."

I just nodded, unable to say anything yet alone think straight. He was strangely nice though his tone was cold. Everything he did was thoroughly thought out and calculated. *What the hell was he planning?*

"Well, I'll leave you to it then. I suppose I don't need to remind you not to leave the house? If you do, I'll know." When I made a face, he continued. "I didn't mean it like that. This is not a prison. You are free to roam as you like. And if there is anything you need, my staff will take care of it."

I nodded again. The phone buzzed in his pocket and he began to scroll through it again. Without another word he rushed out the room, leaving me there standing, wondering if I'll be spending my wedding night alone. *What am I thinking? Of course I want to spend it alone. There is no way I'll let Jax in my bed, even if it's our wedding night.*

The door downstairs slammed shut and after carefully listening in for any other sounds, I determined I was completely and utterly alone. Doing a small victory dance, I pranced to the bathroom, shimmied out of my dress and kicked the door close.

The warm shower was a welcome feeling strumming on my sensitive skin. I spent a long time under the steam, scrubbing the thick makeup off so I could examine my injuries. The freshest ones were still screaming red and throbbing.

Stepping out of the shower, I quickly wrapped myself in a robe and avoided looking at myself in the mirror. I knew the horror that would stare back at me and I didn't need a visual reminder to know it would take a long time to recover.

Jax's had a variety of neat, tailored and expensive clothes but I was happily surprised when I found a drawer full of sweatpants and t-shirts. It was not a surprise however that everything was a shade of gray or black. The clothes smelled just like him.

Mentally exhausted and my body aching, I crawled under the sheets, cuddled up with pillows and dozed off in minutes. Not even the wind howling behind the windows could keep me awake. If only Jackal could have stayed out of my dreams, my sleep would have been more peaceful.

Louisa came by my room once I had awakened. I assumed she gestured to me to have breakfast but if I was honest with myself I could not bring myself to eat one bite even if I wanted to. My mind was too occupied with the recent events. She straightened the room, picked up my wedding dress and made herself scarce. I figured out we would get along just fine.

Chapter 3

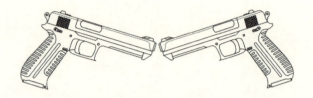

If Jax or anyone else came to the house I didn't see them which I was thankful for. The snowstorm let out eventually and I was able to peer down the window to see the snow covered city buzz with life. The window behind the vanity became my favorite spot to hide in. I spent my days lounging in nothing but a large t-shirt and sweatpants and scrolling endlessly on my phone on social media.

After three days of snacking on nothing but fruit I got from Louisa, I finally caved in and decided to seek out proper food. The house was quiet and dark. My stomach was screaming at me and I felt slightly dizzy climbing down the stairs, my knees shaking with each step. *Why does he have three floors in this stupid house anyway?* Cursing my own stubbornness I tiptoed into the kitchen, opened the fridge and began to rummage through its contents.

I found a bottle of freshly squeezed orange juice and poured myself a glass immediately to sip on while cracking open the various containers of prepped meals. Mentally I scolded myself for not trying them out sooner since the house came with a personal chef that had prepped all these delicious looking foods. *Would it be bad if I tried a little bit of everything? Is that meatloaf?*

I must have been too occupied with the meals since I didn't hear the approaching footsteps and a gun safety being clicked off. Only when the light flicked on, did I finally turn to find myself staring at the barrel of a gun.

"Put your hands up!" A man in black shouted.

On instinct I dropped the glass I was holding and grabbed a handful of knives from the block. The glass shattered at my feet just as I threw the first knife that would have landed square in his eye had he not ducked behind the counter. The gun went off with a bang making my ears ring. The bullet flew just below my ear as I flung another knife to knock the gun out of their hand. I hissed when something stung my sole just as I threw another knife in his direction.

"Stop!" He shouted from his cover as I flung another knife near his head. "Put the knives down!"

"Put the gun down, *mudak*!" Holding up the knife I readied myself for a strike. Training with multiple combat knives I knew exactly where to aim and how fast. My favorite to use was a pair of karambits but the chef knife would have to do in this situation. I flipped it in my hand directing the pointy end towards the shooter. "Now, or I swear I'll gut you like a fish."

"I'm already bleeding you fucking bitch, put the knife down!"

"What the fuck is going on?!" My eyes flew across the kitchen to find my husband standing at the doorway with an army behind him, all holding their guns up at me. The kitchen was a mess. There were glass shards everywhere and blood splattered across the tiles, like a murder scene.

He didn't seem phased at all, but instead walked calmly towards the counter and looked down at the man and the blood covered knife discarded on the floor. "Wilson? Report."

"She got my fucking hand, boss." *Boss? Well that explains how he got into the house but not why he attacked me. I knew I had to be wary of my husband but I wasn't expecting everyone else to want me dead as well.* "Bitch, you're dead! You hear me? Fucking dead."

"I'd like to see you try. Next time I'll cut your fucking tongue and feed it to my dogs!" Not a completely empty threat since father kept a pack of Huskies at our lodge and a Toy in the city, but I wasn't going to tell him that. My heart was drumming so fast it was hard to think straight.

I watched as Jackal crouched down, took the knife and to my shock stabbed Wilson in front of everyone. Over and over the knife entered his body, spraying and spilling the coppery syrup everywhere. He wiped the knife on his shirt and then calmly stood up, snapping his fingers at the other men. His face was void of emotions as he stalked towards me, knife still in hand.

"See to his wounds. I need him at the party tomorrow."

I kept my knife up and watched as he stepped over the glass and into my space. The blade pressed on his throat but he simply put his bloodied knife back on the block. Then he proceeded to take my throwing knife and put it next to the first one. When he didn't make an attempt to remove my last defense, I felt slightly relieved.

"Oh and just so we are clear, Wilson, next time you or anyone else calls my wife a bitch, I'll be the one cutting out your tongue. Understand?" *Swoon.*

His actions and words made me weak in the knees that had nothing to do with my hunger. Twisted as it may be,

Jax looked sexy as hell covered in blood, like the death incarnate, the devil he was known as.

Gurgling sounds came from the man's direction as he was dragged away bleeding profusely all over the polished floor. Jax's eyes never left mine as he spoke to his men. His expression was hard to read and I wasn't sure if he was angry or impressed.

"Is this how you and your men are going to treat me? Am I to expect a bullet to my head for leaving my room?"

"You are quite dramatic for a woman of your caliber."

"Excuse me? Dramatic? He tried to kill me."

"And out of the two of you, he is the one getting stitches tonight. Are you hurt?"

"Uh.. no. I'm fine." A lie that didn't sound believable even to myself.

He took my hand and moved the knife off his throat but didn't make an attempt to remove it from my grasp. Certain that he could've easily disarmed me, that move seemed oddly soothing. Crouching down, he picked me up with one big swoop and proceeded to carry me upstairs like a sack of potatoes.

"What the hell are you doing? Let go of me."

"Your feet are bleeding. Please don't create more mess for Louisa to clean before the party tomorrow. She will bring my coffee cold as a protest."

"Serves you right for treating your wife like this. Put me down." He was surprisingly strong, carrying me up the stairs without getting winded. He didn't seem to be affected at all when he finally placed me on top of the vanity and crouched down to rummage through the cupboards. He emerged with the medkit I had been using to bind my injuries. "I could have stabbed you." I hissed.

"But you didn't, which I'm thankful for. Now stay still

while I look at your feet."

"Seriously I'm fine. Ouch!" I was not fine. The adrenaline had worn off and the sting from earlier turned out to be a huge piece of glass stuck to the bottom of my foot; and it hurt like a motherfucker. I cursed in my native tongue which only made Jax's chuckle as he tended to my feet.

His touch was yet again tender. I watched as his warm hands carefully removed all the shards, softly pressed alcohol swipes to clean the wounds and wrapped them up in bandages.

When he was done, there was a moment of silence as he stood in front of me with his hands in his pockets. I couldn't help but admire how handsome he looked despite being covered in blood. *What would I give to strip him right now? No. What am I thinking? Stop that.*

"I'm sorry for Wilson. He didn't know." He said, his tone low. I sensed a hint of humility and regret, though his expression hadn't changed.

"I'm sorry too, you know, for the hand."

"Don't be. You were just defending yourself and he was doing his job. I'd be fucking disappointed if he didn't try and charge an intruder. I can only assume he thought you were a squatter."

"A squatter in a penthouse?"

"It's a nice house. People have squatted for a lot less." A smile tugged at the corner of my lips. It was out right criminal this man was both handsome and funny at the same time.

"Thank you, by the way, for what you said."

"Don't think nothing of it. Just a simple fact. You are my wife. Even if it's just temporary."

His words stung even though I knew them to be true.

It didn't mean anything. I didn't mean anything *to him*, he just had to keep me alive till the deal was done. Then he could get rid of me. For some reason that thought bothered me more than it should have.

"Anyway, tomorrow I'm hosting a New Years eve party for all of my employees. I'm going to introduce you to them all so there is no mistake in who you are."

"Fine." In my current condition I wasn't keen on parading around all evening but for the sake of keeping the peace between us I had no choice but to comply. I could keep up with the appearances for another night.

"Can you walk?"

"Yes. I'll be fine." Another white lie. It was becoming a habit. I was far from fine, but I had caused enough trouble as it was. And Jax had been surprisingly kind to me. I'd hate to see that change. With a mask of false smile, I hopped off the vanity, suppressing the pain on my feet. "I'll be good as new with just a little sleep." *Unlikely.*

"Then I'll see you tomorrow. Good night, Katy."

"Night. Jax." A flutter of hope began to build in my stomach. Maybe, just maybe Jax was different from what I was expecting. And maybe my marriage to him would be uneventful from now on. Maybe I wouldn't hate staying here indefinitely and for once I wouldn't have to fear the inevitable abuse of a man.

Chapter 4

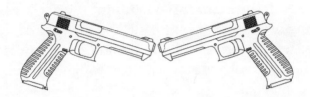

T rue to his words Jax did get most of my things
from my father's residence delivered to his
penthouse. I was happy to have an assortment
of my own clothes though I did enjoy the scent from Jax's
clothes. The t-shirt and sweatpants I never gave back to
him and he never asked for them either.

My bruises were still visible and had turned into an
ugly shade of green and purple. I did my best covering
them with make-up as I got ready for the evening. A
glittering blue velvet dress that reminded me of the night
sky was the only one with sleeves long enough to cover
the rest of the healing wounds.

I adjusted my make-up accordingly, put on some
jewelry and the best formal shoes I'd be able to walk in
even with the cuts on my soles. An agonizing task no
doubt but I was already used to enduring vast amounts
of pain on a daily basis. One evening was child's play
compared to the things I had been through in the past.

There was a knock on the door and when I went to open
it, I was reminded just how handsome Jax was. I shouldn't

have been that easily aroused but the man wore suits like a second skin and had his hair gelled back which made him look absolutely gorgeous.

"Are you ready?" *Don't I look ready?* His eyes traveled up and down my body, but when he didn't comment on my appearance I assumed my outfit was acceptable attire for the evening. I wasn't fishing for compliments but at least acknowledgement for my efforts would have been nice. However his face remained unchanged.

"Yes." I sighed and tugged on the sleeves.

"Good. Let's get this over with."

We descended the stairs and were immediately greeted with the house staff, most whom I was already familiar with. Emilio the chef had prepared a buffet of appetizers, mountains of different hors d'oeuvres and cocktails. *Is that a salmon puff?* Louisa was being her usual self fuzzing about some stains on the coffee table.

In a short amount of time the penthouse had transformed from the white and sterile to a glittering extravaganza. Streamers and balloons gathered up in the ceiling and every surface was covered in silver.

Jax proceeded to mingle amongst the other patrons, greeting and well wishing each one with a handshake, myself in tow. He introduced me to each member of his staff, guards and all, personally ensuring no more incidents would occur because of a misunderstanding. I was theirs to protect with their life.

I saw trayfulls of food being served around but I didn't have time to grab one piece as I was dragged along to meet yet another associate. Putting on my best socialite smile I greeted them politely but stayed quiet during the conversation. It was the best way to keep out of trouble as my mouth tended to have a mind of its own. Instead I focused on spinning the ring on my finger.

"To another successful year, Mr. O'Hara." A man with a large mustache said toasting his glass. "And congratulations on the new bride."

I nodded my head politely as a response.

"We thank you. Looking forward to spending a new year with her." He said it so naturally yet I could sense the coldness in those words. We hadn't spent any time together these past days. Not that I expected to either. I was just amazed how my marriage wasn't so different that of my parents, once upon a time.

They too kept up appearances to the public, fabricated images to the paparazzi of a perfect marriage, yet behind closed doors it was far from perfect. If it was any regular marriage, I assumed my mother would have left long ago and filed for a divorce. But we were no regular people. When you marry into a crime family, there is only one way to leave. In a casket. The creed demanded it.

Nodding and smiling agreeingly was becoming slightly tedious and pretentiously annoying. Every step was agonizing, every handshake rattling my already aching body and the hunger in my stomach only grew each passing minute.

Another tray passed by. *Crab cakes. I'd kill for a handful and some dip right now. Who am I kidding, I'd settle for just one bite. I shouldn't have skipped breakfast for the fourth time this week.* I had only myself to blame for my poor condition. Except for last night, that was on Wilson. During the whole conflict I completely forgot about my dinner and went to bed hungry.

I think I mumbled an excuse before hobbling to the bathroom and locking the door. The room was spinning. Anchoring myself against the sink, I splashed some water on my face in an attempt to alleviate some of the dizziness. Before I knew it, everything went dark and the last thing I remembered was feeling the cold tile against my cheek.

At some point, I was awakened by an annoying beeping sound going off somewhere above my head. My eyelids were heavy, my mouth was like sand and there was a steady pounding in my head. Somehow I couldn't feel the rest of my body, no aches, no pains, no irritations to my injuries. I was under a cover of some sort that was warm and soft, and I definitely wasn't wearing the midnight gown anymore.

Willing my eyes open the first thing I saw was bright lights. *Someone turn that shit off right now.* I groaned and made an attempt to crawl from under whatever the thing I was under. The task was laborious, every muscle and nerve in my body was fighting against me to stay down. *Ugh.* Simply moving my head was overbearingly taxing.

After what seemed like a century, my eyes adjusted to the light and I could finally scan my surroundings. The beeping was coming from a monitor connected to multiple wires that were attached to me. On my other side was a pole with a bag of liquid, a drip and an IV running down to my arm. *Well shit, how hard did I fall?* Sitting up I could tell that I was in a hospital room. Everything smelled like hand sanitizer and plastic, even the thing I was wearing smelled sterile.

I swung my legs over the edge of the bed and reached for the glass of water on the nightstand. The cords attached to me tugged and pulled as I stretched my arm towards the table just out of my reach. *Damn it. Fuck this.* Digging into my hospital gown, I found the pads connecting me to the machine and yanked them clean off one by one. The monitor went quiet, *finally*, and I was able to stand up, get a hold of the glass and extinguish my thirst.

"What the fuck are you doing out of bed?" Voice belonging to Jax growled behind me. Spinning around I almost spilled the remaining contents of the glass all over myself.

"I-I'm sorry. I just-"

"Sit your ass down."

As if struck by lightning, I did as I was told and backed up against the edge of the bed. Jax strode across the floor and stopped right in front of me, crossing his arms and smelling like a fresh shower. *Damn, I want to lick him so bad.* Shocked at my lewd thoughts I had to physically shake my head and take a deep breath to calm myself. Jax's eyes narrowed and there was a rumble in his chest, so I bowed my head down banishing the idea of tasting him, willing my mind to focus on anything else.

"H-have you been here the entire time?" A daring question I happened to blurt out before I had a chance to stop myself.

"No." He didn't hesitate. He gave me a straight answer with that monotone voice of his I had gotten used to. Of course he wouldn't just stay here. He was a busy man after all. To think he would even spare a moment with his wife in the hospital made my chest ache. *I'm not his real wife anyway. Just a fake one till he can get rid of me. Why would he care?*

"Right." I fiddled with the wrinkles on the gown trying to smooth them out like it would help me smooth out the wrinkles in my mind.

"I had a few errands to run today. You should be in bed and stay there. Doctor's orders." Remaining on the edge, I frowned at him. *Doctor's orders my ass.*

"I'm fine."

"Your lies sting. Makes me believe I can not properly take care of my wife. After all, have I not provided you with everything you could possibly desire?"

"You have."

"And have I not been accommodating enough to assure your comfort and safety?"

"Yes, but-"

"And have I not been perfectly clear of the terms of our agreement?"

"Uh. I suppose."

"Then what the fuck is your problem? Are you so high up on your pedestal that you can't comprehend the simplest thing as to keep yourself out of harm's way?"

"High up? No. It's not like that." I did not dare to look him in the eyes. His voice had risen till he was almost roaring with anger.

"Oh? Then explain to me why I got arrested because the doctor who examined you, saw the condition of your body and reported me for domestic abuse and assault I knew nothing about. Took me hours and a few good lawyers to prove I had nothing to do with your injuries."

I sat there quietly, taking in all that he had to say. I was still haunted by the ghost of my father, feeling his touch on my skin, his hands on my neck and his boots on my back. I had been branded, bruised and scarred countless times and countless times after and yet my heart ached knowing my troubles had now burdened someone else.

"I didn't mean to upset you, husband. I'm sorry." I said, stilling the quiver in my voice. The ring offered me little comfort as it was a shiny reminder of the contract I had signed.

"Sorry? That's it? That's all you have to say, that you are sorry?"

"What do you want me to say?" I shrugged, letting out a long breath. Jax remained stern.

"Tell me who the fuck did this to you?"

"I-" My head fell between my shoulders. A pang of pain struck my heart. I knew revealing my father as the perpetrator would have catastrophic consequences. Going against my father meant going against the entire Gregorovich empire. It would start a war. *Literally.* I couldn't allow that to happen. "Doesn't matter anymore. What's done is done."

"It matters to me! It's not done until whomever touched you bleeds. I will cut them till there is no more blood to spill and their corpse lays cold on the bottom of the river. Tell me."

His choice of words made my stomach flutter. Fear mixed with arousal caused my whole body to shudder. His eyes were full of fire and determination which was exhilarating. But there was still a part of me that was unsure if he was being truthful, so I shook my head.

"You don't understand. There is nothing you can do."

"There is nothing I *can't do* concerning my wife. Now, tell me the truth or do I have to kill every last one who has ever even laid their eyes upon you before you tell me?"

"This is madness. Can't you just let it go?"

"No. Why do you insist on protecting those who hurt you?"

"Because it wouldn't matter. You can't protect me from what already happened. Nobody can."

A long silence followed where I counted the tiles on the floor and he stood there seething. Eventually he left without saying another word, slamming the door behind him. Feeling my throat close up I crawled into a ball and hugged my knees. I felt like I needed to cry but I couldn't bring myself to tears. *If being alone meant nobody could hurt me, then why was I hurting?* I asked myself drifting off to sleep.

Hours later, when I was brought back to the house, I was happy to be in my own clothes and in a room where everything wasn't wrapped in plastic. The doctor ensured my fainting was caused by mild malnourishment and dehydration. *My own stupidity really.* They gave me medication for the pain and anxiety, as well as a little advice on how to relieve some of the stress I had been experiencing. It included aromatherapy and getting massages. *As if. But of course I have been stressed lately. I'm married to a murderous psychopath.*

"You will stay in your room till further notice. You are not to leave the penthouse for any reason. Guards have been instructed to stay by your side at all times. No exceptions. I will have you under surveillance 24/7."

"You said this wasn't a prison."

"I will make it one if I need to. I'm not arguing this. You will stay here where you are safe."

"No." That was the first time I truly disagreed with Jax. Even though I hadn't exactly taken advantage of going out freely, I still didn't like the idea of not having the option at all. *No. I don't want to be trapped. Anything but that.*

Images flooded my mind, filling it with memories of my father locking me in the basement for punishment. Vague flashes of a small child clawing at a door, crying till her voice died, begging and pleading for anyone to come and save her. Nobody came. Not once. I shook my head banishing the thoughts and faced the demon in front of me.

"No, please. You can't do that. Please don't do this. I can't stay here like this."

"Try to run and I will have to drag you back in here, kicking and screaming, but bring you back I will non the less; and I swear, I won't be as accommodating anymore. Am I clear?" His voice rumbled in his chest as he strode across the room to get to me. I thought his deep, low, calm voice was even more threatening than when he was shouting.

"Jax, please." His hand tugged at the base of my neck, bundling my hair in his fist and angling my head so I couldn't shake no to him anymore. It wasn't painful, but stern enough, letting me know just how serious he was. I swallowed, silencing the whimper that lingered on my lips.

"Am I clear?" The mint on his breath invaded my nostrils as he leaned in closer, daring me to defy him again. He had never been like this towards me before but I was convinced he only acted nice to lull me into false security. He was the devil after all. As my fight proved to be futile, I finally admitted defeat.

"Crystal." He held me like that for a moment longer before releasing me, brushing his thumb over my jaw. I mentally threw daggers at his back as he stalked across the room, closed the door behind him and locked me in. Guess the conversation was over and my confinement had begun.

Chapter 5

I can't say January was particularly enjoyable for me. For the first week I wasn't allowed to leave my room at all. To my irritation, guards were positioned at my door day and night in rotating shifts, one inside and another outside of the room. I was never alone.

They even attempted to follow me to the bathroom but after threatening to parade in the nude in front of everyone, Jax caved and let me bathe in peace. Sort of. From then on, he saw to me personally everytime I needed to take a shower, no guards allowed. He set up a chair outside the bathroom facing directly at the shower, swearing to me he was doing it for my protection and was only going to look, not touch.

At first I was embarrassed and shy stripping down in front of him, but knowing he could only see me vaguely through the fogged up glass gave me at least a little protection. I was still seething, but in my solidarity, I had plenty of time planning his demise, imagining all the ways I could torture him.

Due to the doctor's orders, I had been given an assortment of therapeutic oils to use in the shower, ranging from camomille to sage. Drizzling the honeyed liquid to my hands, the smell of lavender filled the room as I lathered it all over my body. I kneaded my muscles, ran my fingers over my cuts and bruises and attended to every bit of my skin all the while Jax watched me silently.

The following week, my anger had subsided and I had grown boulder, more daring in the shower. I massaged my neck and breasts, pinched my hardening nipples and circled them long and intensively. A moan rippled out of my lips as my hand traveled past my stomach and over my mound. Using my fingers, I parted my lips and dipped them inside my already needy pussy. It had been too long since the last time I had come.

Despite Jax's best efforts to act like my movements didn't affect him, I could tell his mask had begun to crack. As I lathered myself with soap, his eyes darkened, following the trail of my hands massaging my breasts. I bit my lip, hiding my satisfaction knowing he was getting hot and bothered in his seat while watching me pleasure myself. I made sure not to spare him from my moans as I came on my fingers. His chair was empty by the time I stepped out of the shower.

In the third week I left the shower door open and put on the show of my life. I was done playing games. I was going to break him. My confinement had remained strict and unrelenting and I desperately needed some air without being watched constantly.

In preparation I had put on the sexiest lingerie I owned made of very thin lace that was almost see through. Jax placed the chair in its usual spot as I slowly got undressed one piece of clothing at a time, starting with the buttons of my shirt. One by one they popped open, revealing more and more of my lace bra hidden underneath. My nipples were already hard and poking small peaks through the fabric.

Jax's gaze hardened, his jaw clenched and I could already see the small twitch in his pants. I was going to torture him in the most delicious way possible. Turning around I threw the shirt to the side, undid the clasp, tossing my bra too and then proceeded to undo my jeans. I made sure to bend low, removing my pants, giving him a good view of my round ass.

His eyes burned a hole in my thong so I made quick work to remove it and hopped in the shower. The water made my skin prickly and my nipples harden even more before I adjusted the temperature. The scent of jasmine filled my nostrils as steam rose in the room. Standing under the rain shower, I began the slow dance on my skin with my fingers.

Knowing Jax was watching me gave me such a rush I could feel it down to my core. Never before had my pussy throbbed with such aching need for a touch, a man's touch, *his* touch.

I rubbed my nipples and massaged my breasts, giving them the attention they had been craving for so long; and I knew Jax was enjoying watching me as I heard a low growl coming from his direction. *Good, keep your eyes on me. Because that's all you ever do, just watch. Coward. I'm going to destroy you.*

Turning to face the wall, I pressed my heated cheek against the tiles and bent over, showing him everything I was doing to myself; wishing it was him. My pussy was slick from my own juices mixing with the water and shower oil, which made it easy to slide my fingers in.

With slow circular motions, I tease my clit while drawing more and more slickness from my opening.

Another pained groan reached my ears and I peered over my shoulder to find Jax, who was biting his fist, unable to tear his eyes away from me. He was so close to his breaking point, I was sure of it. He was stroking his cock through his pants, clearly showing the effect I had on him. I pulled my fingers out of my pussy and brought them to my lips, tasting my own juices.

The chair flew backwards with a clang and Jax's hands were on me a second later. He pressed me against the tiles with his body and I felt his hands wrap around my torso, cupping my breasts. His mouth was everywhere. He was all lips, teeth and tongue, tasting me for the first time in weeks. It was like fireworks had lit up my skin. A moan left my lips as he sucked on the sensitive flesh on my neck, sending shivers down my spine.

"Mmh, what are you doing to me, wife?" He murmured next to my ear, his voice all husky and full of lust. I felt every vibration of his words, like a tantalizing wave playing with my senses. It was just like I remembered it and more.

"Nothing. *You* are touching *me*." A voice not my own answered, breathy and shaken. His hands had laid claim on my nipples, pinching and rolling them between his fingers like two little pearls they were. I hardly recognized the woman I had become, so needy, so desperate for him.

"As if you haven't been teasing me this entire time *begging* for me to touch you. To *pleasure* you." His hands moved lower, following the contours of my curves as if to memorize every dip and slope of my hips and ass, leaving trails of goosebumps in their wake. The shower did nothing to ease the sensation left on my skin.

"And what if I have?" His body engulfed me. He didn't seem to care that his clothes were completely soaked from the shower and it turned me on even more. Him fully clothed and me completely naked in front of him. "You don't want me anyway."

"Is that what *you* want, *dear wife*, to be pleased? To be *touched*?" His hands caressed my back, ass and thighs without going anywhere near where I needed him the most. He made sure his fingers never came closer than an inch from my pussy. And if only he had moved just a little further, he would have known just how badly I wanted him to touch me; how wet I was for him. "To be fucked?"

"Yes." The word flew out of my mouth before I had a chance to catch myself. He was playing me, skillfully so and I was putty in his hands. Within minutes I had become needy and wanting all because of his attentive touch and low rumbling voice. His actions were every bit as commanding as were his words. "Please."

"Hmm, how could I deny my wife pleasure when you ask so nicely?"

With one hand, he gathered my hair in his fist and pulled me towards him, forcing me to arch my back. My ass protruded out and grinded against his erection, earning me another growl from Jax. A slap echoed on the walls along with my voice as Jax brought down his hand, branding my ass cheek with his print. The skin felt scorched, but just as the tingling soothed down, he did it again, and again and again, till I was mewling with pain mixed with pleasure.

"Fuck. I could get used to seeing my marks on you. You look absolutely gorgeous with my hand right here." He traced the outline of the heated print on my ass, settling the pain. It sounded like he was enjoying it. I sounded like a mess, heaving against the tile, shivering and shaking with anticipation for the next one, knowing my pussy was completely soaked and not because of the shower raining down on us. "Should I stop?"

"Yes. I mean no. I- ah!" Another strike connected with my cheek making it jiggle. He left his hand on my skin, feeling the print that was forming on it like a signature. He was marking me as his. "Jax. I'm begging you."

"Begging for what, Katy? I would love to paint my marks all over this sexy body of yours."

I peered over my shoulder to look at him as he trailed off. He seemed to be admiring the handprint he had left on my skin next to the old scars made by my father. With one finger he traced the white lines on my back and counted them silently. Something in the moment had shifted and his mood suddenly changed. For the first time his stoic expression was gone, replaced by something resembling remorse.

"No one else will lay their hands on you ever again. I'll fucking kill them. Every single one that has ever hurt you will be dead."

"You don't think they are hideous?" I said turning to face him. Water cascaded down his dark hair in small droplets, drizzling onto my face as his heated stare scorched my skin. He seemed to search for more marks, which I knew there would be plenty, all over my arms, legs and torso. His fingers touched the branding scar on my chest I had covered with a tattoo years ago in memory of my mother.

"I could never think you are hideous." His hands wrapped around me as his lips fell on my chest, right where the ink was. With a moan, I surrendered to his mercy as his lips danced on my skin, kissing and sucking everywhere he could reach. The closer he got to my mouth, the more urgent the kisses became.

In this ravenous heat, I peeled off his wet shirt, tossing it somewhere in the room while placing a trail of kisses on his pecs and abs. He was covered in ink, more than I had scars, and it made him look sexy as hell. I made a mental note to one day discover them all. But I was in a frenzy and needed some release.

"What are you doing?"

"You've seen all of me. Now I want to see you." I slid down to my knees, letting my hands travel along his body, stopping at his belt. "Hold still."

"Are you giving me orders, wife?"

"You can stop me at any point if you don't like it." I raised my brow and gave him a little smirk as my fingers made quick work on his buckle loosening his belt. His pants came down a little with a tug, revealing black boxers that left zero for the imagination. He was large, just like I had imagined it, and the fabric was barely able to hold his erection.

My fingers dug under the wristband and pulled down, releasing his dick from its confinement. Immediately I was enthralled by the sheer size of it, complemented with veins and-.

"It's pierced? Wow. I've never seen one before." Leaning in, I placed a kiss next to the piercing and licked my way up all the way to the tip. I could feel Jax's body tremble, and looking up, I noticed he was leaning against the tile, shielding me from the downpour. *How can this conflicting man be so thoughtful?*

I did it again, slowly licking along his full length, trailing his veins with my tongue and circling the tip, finally sucking it in my mouth. He tasted salty and a little bit like the shower oils. I slid in as much as I could of his length and moaned when the velvety tip hit the back of my throat. The vibrations caused Jax to curse out and thrust his hips forward, sinking his cock even deeper.

My eyes watered. I could barely breathe. But I refused to gag, letting him think I couldn't handle his size. Pulling out, he thrust in again, grinding the piercing along my tongue. He repeated the motion over and over again till I was a blubbering mess and covered in drool mixed with his precum. Sensing his climax approaching, I wrapped both of my hands around his cock and began pumping, slowly mimicking the rhythm with my mouth.

"Fuck. Don't stop." Jax grunted above me, leaning his head against the tiles. With his hands, he guided my actions, leading me to work at a rapid pace. There was no way I was stopping now.

His breaths became shallow. I kept one hand on his cock, rubbing him with a tight grasp and let the other one fall down to my pussy.

Spreading my lips, I felt the overwhelming slickness dripping out of it, soaking my fingers so I could easily rub circles around my swollen clit. I was so turned on I knew I was close to my orgasm and based on the ragged sounds above me, so was Jax. His body had gone rigid. He groaned, fisting my hair as I milked his cock even faster.

I worked my fingers deeper into my pussy, thrusting them in and out in the same rhythm as I did rubbing his cock. With one last jerk of his hips, he shot hot cum in my mouth, roaring from the power of his orgasm. Soon after I reached my own climax and moaned in pleasure with his cock still in my mouth.

When he finally pulled away and released me from his grasp, the cum spilled out of my mouth and dribbled down my jaw. Jax panted heavily, sliding down the wall to join me on the floor. The rain shower felt like a warm drizzle washing away the mess we had created.

"Where the hell did you learn to do that?"

"I don't think you want to know." I leaned my head back and closed my eyes wanting to bask in the afterglow for a moment longer.

"You're probably right. I might have to kill every single one that has ever done that with you, too."

"It's for the best. I don't even remember half of them."

I swallowed down the chuckle thinking someone would be jealous of the people I had slept with in the past, people that didn't matter anymore, people that hadn't left a lasting expression.

"Besides, you can't go off killing everyone who has had something to do with me in my lifetime. It would be a massacre and outright impossible."

"Is that a challenge?"

"No. Please don't go killing people just because you can."

"Well now you are putting me in a hard spot, wife. Killing is part of my job. It's what I do and I'm fucking good at it."

"So I've heard."

I didn't want to think about how many of the rumors were true. Jackal O'Hara gained his status, not simply by being the son of Mathias O'Hara, but by killing his way to the top. I heard he claimed his first victim at the age of thirteen and single handedly killed the West village cartel by the age of 17.

After a while, he got up, turned off the shower, pulled me off the floor and he proceeded to discard the wet clothes. The ink on his thighs was only visible for a few seconds before he wrapped his waist in a towel, leaving me curious.

"Look, I think we had a really bad start to this whole marriage thing." I said, wrapping myself in a robe, leaning against the sink.

"I agree. Just because we don't like each other doesn't mean we can't at least try to get along and somewhat tolerate one another."

"Umh, yeah. I'd like that." I nodded.

He gathered his things and walked out of the bathroom as I trailed after him. The cold air of the room was a harsh contrast on my skin compared to the steam we had just been in. I followed Jax to my door where he stopped to look back at me as we said our goodbyes. His fresh out of the shower look was deliriously sexy, and had I not just cum, I might have asked him to stay for longer.

"Oh and for the record, I don't *don't* like you."

I closed the door, giving Jax one final look letting him know I meant what I said. Despite our rough start and against my better judgment, I had let Jax closer than I initially thought I would. I just hope it wouldn't end up costing me more than I was ready to bargain for.

Chapter 6

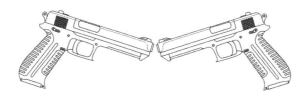

T ruly I didn't believe how things could change just after one conversation. My house arrest was lifted and I was permitted to go down to the city while heavily guarded. I didn't, but it was nice to know I had the option to do so if I so desired. I had no reason to, as Jax had everything provided for me and I was all too happy to hibernate through the cold season.

Jax was busy most of the time, sometimes being gone for days or even weeks on end and when he did return to the house, I was already fast asleep and he'd be gone before I woke up. Regardless, we had gotten into the habit of texting each other when we had the chance. Mostly innocent. I'd tell him about my day and share small details of my life prior. He obviously couldn't tell me as much of his day due to the delicacy of his work, which I understood.

However sometimes the texts turned a little bit more naughty and erotic. He'd send me a message saying how he missed seeing me in the shower naked and I would send him a pic of myself wearing the skimpiest lingerie I owned to tease him. This was something I'd never done with anyone else before and it felt exhilarating, to the point I ended up masturbating every day just imagining all the kinky things I wanted to do with him upon his return.

I had just gotten out of my nightly shower, laid down in bed and turned the light off when my phone buzzed on the nightstand. The screen lit up with Jax's name as the incoming call. Hastily I swiped right to answer. It was past midnight which meant it was early morning where he was.

"Hey. Did I wake you?" Surprisingly I was delighted to hear his voice. It had a warmth to it which didn't exist there before.

"Mhh no, I was just turning in." Sitting up, I turned the light back on so I could stay awake during our conversation. I didn't want to miss out on him more than I already was. A thought I didn't think could be possible; missing him.

"Are you alone?"

"Of course. Why'd you ask?"

Honestly, as great as my bodyguards were, they weren't much for a company and the staff was usually busy all day. As strange as it was, I wouldn't have minded some alone time with my husband. At least I'd have someone to talk to.

"Because I got you a gift."

"You know you don't have to get me anything. I'm quite content."

"Yes, I'm aware, but I thought you might like it and I asked Louisa to hide it for you when you weren't looking."

Butterflies took flight in my stomach. I hadn't gotten a gift in a long time. Ever since mom had died, we never exchanged gifts, never celebrated birthdays or christmas like we used to. It hadn't been the same anymore. I had no room to complain, though. My life was privileged, spoiled with the luxuries of a bratva princess, but I never got what I truly craved more than anything.

"Should I look for it?" My eyes were already darting around the room pondering where one would hide a gift. Nothing seemed out of the ordinary.

"If you want it then yes. Hurry. Put the phone down and start searching. I'll wait."

I threw the covers off and flung myself off the bed in an instant. My first thought was my wardrobe, but after a thorough five minutes of searching I couldn't find anything out of place. Next I rummaged around the bathroom but came out empty handed. The last place I searched was under the bed and when even that was fruitless, I had a creeping suspicion I was being played at.

"Are you sure there is a gift or is this some sort of trick?" I asked, grabbing my phone and sitting down on the bed again.

"Positive. I picked it out for you personally."

"I feel silly asking but how big is it? Just so I know what to look for."

"Not big." There was a moment of pause on the other end before I heard Jax speak again. "It should fit in your hand."

I felt like I had already searched everywhere. There was no place in my room I hadn't already searched. *Unless.* Skipping across the room, I peered into the dark hallway and after finding it empty, tiptoed towards the large doors at the end of the hallway.

Jax's room was dark and dramatic, just like him. The tall charcoal walls dominated the mostly sophisticated and modern atmosphere. A large steel frame bed with dark satin linens faced the floor to ceiling windows overlooking the city. And there was a box on top of his bed.

"I think I found it."

"Good. Open it." Switching the phone on speaker, I placed it on top of his night stand and sat on his bed with the box in my lap.

Like a kid on Christmas, I ripped the tape, unraveled the packing material and dug into the box only to find another box within. Smooth red velvet tickled my fingertips as I followed the golden trim of the box to the clasp. I held my breath as I opened it and discovered some sort of plastic sculpture.

"Oh it's cute. What is it?"

"Take off your panties."

"Um what?"

"You heard me. Take them off and place the gift between your legs."

"I-" My cheeks burned as I turned the thing in my hand to find two small buttons on the surface. "Umh, so it's like a vibrator?"

"Yes, but only I can control it."

" Wait? Are you serious? How?"

"It works with my phone. Now hurry. My patience has its limits, wife."

I've never undressed as quickly as I did at that moment. I climbed on top of his bed properly, laid down and placed the toy between my legs just like he had instructed. At first it felt cold against my pussy lips, making me jolt, but soon adjusted to my body temperature as I buried it between my thighs. Pressing on one of the buttons, the device hummed to life with a low vibration against my lips.

"Are you ready?"

"Yes."

The first burst of vibrations had my head flying off the pillow as I gasped at the sudden change of rhythm. It started off hard but rolled into a slow rumble like a wave. Over and over again he hit me with the wave building up my orgasm. My hands automatically reached to massage my breasts to add to the stimulation.

"Ahh. Fuck." I hissed.

"Don't hold back your sounds. I want to hear your voice. I need to hear how much you're enjoying this."

He increased the frequency of the waves to match my shallow inhales and moans as I plunged myself deeper into the mattress chasing the high. My back arched with each jolt I received through the toy vibrating on my clit, every pulse stronger than the last.

"Oh god." Trashing in the sheets, I was unable to withhold the sounds coming out of my mouth. The pulse rippled over my clit, drawing my eyes closed, as I drifted off to the sweet sensation of bliss.

Giving control to someone else over your body like that had never crossed my mind before. It was thrilling and exciting and totally unexpected. With all logic I should have been more resentful giving my consent so easily, but I turned out feeling more empowered instead. The lack of control gave me the freedom to simply enjoy the sensations Jax was creating in my body; and his name flew out of my lips just as easily.

"That's it. Tell me how good it feels." His voice rumbled from the phone, saying all the right things, coaxing my orgasm to crest.

The device hummed loudly as he traced the app

controls with a circular motion that mirrored against my pussy. My clit had become a sensitive little pearl, trembling under the swollen hood. I guess Jax heard my whimpering as he turned the vibration on even higher, putting pressure exactly where I needed it.

"So good. Just like that." He stayed silent as he played expertly with my clit, bringing me to the edge of oblivion and then holding me there. "Jax, please. I'm so close."

I could hardly breathe, drawing in shallow breaths, tethering at the verge of my orgasm. The feeling began to build from the tips of my toes and rolled over my body like a shock wave, sparking at my every nerve. And just as I thought I would explode, the buzzing stopped abruptly and the feeling died down. Sucking air back into my lungs, I expressed my immediate disappointment by sobbing to the phone. *Jerk.*

"Ah-aah. You can't cum just yet." I squeezed my thighs together, pressing the toy harder onto my pussy in hopes to alleviate the edge of my denied orgasm. "Be patient."

The toy turned on again, this time more slowly, steadily vibrating against my pussy and starting the build up yet again. My legs were shaking trying to hold the toy in place when the pulse became harder, more demanding. I cried out sinking deeper into the mattress just as the pulses pushed me to the edge.

"Jax. I'm gonna-"

He turned the vibration off again earning him an earful of my desperate moans. I felt almost feverish being so close to my climax and being denied the release right at its peak. I cursed out in my native tongue as a frantic plea for Jax to end my misery and give me the orgasm I deserved.

"Please. I'm begging you. I can't take much more of

this."

"You can. Just wait a little longer."

"You are killing me."

"So dramatic, little wife." Jax mocked through the phone. *He is truly a cruel man.*

I felt my heart skip a beat when the vibrations returned to my skin, hard and rapidly. My clit was sensitive due to the vigorous teasing and I was certain I wouldn't be able to handle much more of it without bursting. Jax was relentless with the device, taunting me, as I writhed crying and moaning between pleasure and pain. When the vibrator died yet again, I thought to finish myself off just to get it over with. I couldn't take another round of denied release. Death would have been more merciful than this delicious torture.

My hands glided over my stomach and in between my legs. The vibrator was hot and slick with my juices. Pressing my fingers through my folds, I could still feel the effects of the toy. My lips were swollen and my clit had me trembling just from the slightest touch. I shuddered, pushing one finger inside my pussy and pumping it in and out a few times.

"Don't you fucking dare touch yourself." Jax growled, but the sound wasn't coming from the phone, but from the doorway. With a gasp, I pushed myself up in a sitting position.

There he was, the devil himself, all six feet of him, looking as menacing as I remembered. The light in the hallway cast a halo around him, hiding his face in the shadows. He slammed the door shut, pulled off his tie and proceeded to discard the suit jacket in the same stride he took to cross the room.

"Jax. What are you doing here? I thought you were still

out of the country." I pulled my legs under me and sat on the pads of my feet, ignoring the throbbing between my legs.

"I was, but I couldn't stop thinking about my poor wife all alone in the penthouse, so I took the jet." His eyes were burning with a mad desire as he licked his lips, hungrily roaming his eyes all over my body. "I was already on my way back from the airport when I called you."

"I can't believe you are here."

"Missed me?"

"No."

"Don't lie, wife. I can see how wet you are." I slammed my legs together but there was no denying how ridiculously turned on I was. Jax kneeled on the bed, pried my thighs open and placed his hand on my pussy. "Are you really going to say no to me? To this?"

"I - ah." He dragged one of his fingers along my slit and my head fell back, relishing in the feeling of his touch. I couldn't help but moan as he dragged his finger over my clit, teasing the already sensitive nub.

"Look at you. So needy for me. I bet I could make you come with just my fingers. Or should I stop?"

The coldness of the air hit me as he removed his hand off my pussy. A voice not my own cried out staring straight into his dark, lustful eyes. I grabbed his hand and pulled it back to my apex.

"Please don't stop. I can't take it anymore." My hips moved on their own, grinding against his hand, making it slick from my arousal. He didn't make any attempts to pull away again but he didn't use his fingers either. I was going mad for his touch. "Please, keep doing that and let me cum."

"Fuck. I do like it when you beg." He pulled me closer.

His other hand snaked its way to my hair and settled at the nape of my neck, just the way I liked it. I felt his hot breath against my skin, making me shiver, as he hovered his lips next to my ear. "Beg harder."

"Ah! Please. Jax, please please please. Make me cum. I need you to make me cum. I'll do anything."

"Now that sounds like a deal I can't refuse." He grinned against my skin, nibbling and sucking his way to my neck.

With one smooth motion, he pulled at my hips, flipping me over so I landed on my back, legs splayed open for his view. My body trembled as he lowered himself, kissing my knee, then my inner thigh, lower and lower, till he was an inch away from my pussy. His breath fanned the curls on my mound and I swear I could feel myself gushing, wetness dripping down my ass.

"Tell you what. I'll make you a deal. For every orgasm I give you, you agree to go out on a date with me. Does that sound good?"

My mind was drawing a blank. I couldn't think of a downside to his suggestion. His absence had been the norm for the better part of our marriage. I had been grateful for the solitude. The thought of anything else besides avoidant in our relationship hadn't even crossed my mind, the casual sexting excluded. The idea of a date night with him seemed so unlike him, yet he was offering it to me so easily.

I had to blink twice to realize I had not given him my answer. He was patiently hovering over my bare pussy.

"Yes." The second that word left my lips, his head had already fallen down.

My eyes rolled into the back of my skull as he closed his mouth over my clit. Masterfully he swirled his tongue over the hood and sucked in ever so slightly. The long

long rounds of teasing and denial had heightened my senses, making me feel every hum of his breath, stroke of his tongue and pressure of his lips stronger and more powerful than I had ever experienced before.

"Oh God."

I think he murmured *'god can't help you now'* against my lips but I was too far gone to make sense of it. Feeling the heat build up, I clung to the sheets, dragging my nails along the fabric and bunching it in my fists. I was so close to the orgasm I knew if he denied me again it would be the death of me. *And then his. I might have to murder him for real.*

I erupted so fast I couldn't breathe for a moment. The room changed colors and I swear I could see stars. My head was spinning and my insides melted, a wave after wave with the most earth shattering orgasm of my life. His tongue swirled around my clit, drawing every last desperate cry and moan out of me, as I convulsed out of control.

Only, he didn't stop. He never stopped touching me. I felt him, kissing my inner thighs and my lower stomach, softly marking my skin with his lips and patiently waiting for my breathing to settle. With a long sigh I indicated my satisfaction.

"Thank you. That was amazing."

"That's one." I must have looked dazed since he added quickly. "You think I was kidding? I meant what I said. Every orgasm I give you, you agree to go out with me. We're not done yet. I plan on banking as many dates as possible. Are you ready?"

My mouth fell open which he took as a yes and dove back down. He dragged his tongue along my slit sucking up the juices left of my orgasm. Tremors ran through my body, like mixed emotions between greed and contentment. I had my release and yet I wanted more. One was not enough but I was afraid my body couldn't handle any more of this torture. Not teasing nor denial.

Jax was far the best pussy eater I've had the *pleasure* of meeting. From all the people I've slept with in the past none of them could even compare to what he was doing to me. With one swoop of his tongue I felt the steady pulse of my climax starting to accumulate in my stomach. My fingers dug into his hair, tugging at the roots and holding him in place.

The second orgasm ripped through me fast when Jax closed his lips over my clit and sucked in hard, vibrating his tongue in rapid succession. My back arched from the mattress but this time Jax hooked his arms around my thighs and pulled me in deeper, unwilling to let me go till I was thoroughly spent.

"That's two." He rasped climbing on top of me. "Round three?"

Hard as I tried, my words slurred and nothing but an incoherent mumble left my lips. I don't believe he heeded my protest. He kissed me ever so gently, letting me taste myself on his tongue. He smelled absolutely delicious; like sweat, cigarettes and aftershave. My fingers made quick work of his buttons, exposing the carved muscles underneath the shirt. I dragged my nails along his ink and felt the heat radiating off his body.

My body melted into him. I fit perfectly laying between his elbows, cradled underneath his torso. He was sweet and erotic. Every move, every touch, every drawn out rumble of his breath was refined; and I couldn't help myself not to admire him from my point of view. When he kissed, he closed his eyes and used his lips and tongue like it was second nature to him. I was surprised he was more known for his skills as a ruthless killer and not as a gentle lover. Or did he not simply leave any witnesses to tell of their experience with him.

"Jax? You aren't going to kill me after this, are you?"

"What makes you think that I will?" He murmured against my skin.

"I don't know. Just the thought that you're like a black widow or something." His body went rigid as he stared back at me, confusion painted all over his face as a small crease appeared between his eyebrows.

"Black widow?"

"You know? Like you fuck 'em and kill 'em without any mercy."

"That's what you're thinking about? Now? Of all the things you could be thinking about, you chose that?" He deepened the kiss and I could feel his massive erection pressing down on my pussy grinding against me. "You're thinking too much. I'm about to change that."

Before I had a chance to reply, his mouth was on mine again, silencing the yelp I made. I felt his fingers pushing through my folds again and dipping inside my pussy. He began pumping them in and out of me, slowly and agonizingly, building up my next orgasm by hitting me in the right spot.

Jax was relentless, using every trick in his book to bring me over the edge over and over again. I barely had a breath between each orgasm and not a moment to recover before he was already drawing out another one. Eventually I blacked out and fell away from the world, sated and utterly spent. I never thought I'd be lulled to sleep by the devil.

Chapter 7

Dictionary says: *Friends with benefits relationships is a term commonly used to reference a relationship that is sexual without being romantic. Typically, these relationships can be between people that consider themselves platonic and friends.*

But Jax and I weren't friends, we barely knew each other. We were married, but only on paper. Two strangers stuck together by default, just because our marriage was beneficial to someone else, someone outside of our legal bonds, which left me wondering, what were we?

Jackal O'Hara was a complicated man. In the daylight he would act aloof, cold and indifferent. I remembered his face, strikingly handsome and carved to the perfection and yet stiff and emotionless when my father announced our engagement. But unlike my father, he wasn't cruel and unkind, just simply distant, allowing me much free time and privacy.

However after our little marathon it seemed he couldn't get enough of me, especially naked. I'd be undressed within minutes of his arrival as he dove to explore every inch of my body with his tongue, like he was imprinting me to his memory. I did my best to return the favor, but Jax's tattoos remained a mystery to me since he stayed mostly clothed during sex.

Being married didn't turn out to be as bad either as I had initially feared. I suppose I got a taste of marital bliss since we got to spend more time together. We went on the dates I owed Jax, *they were many,* like concerts, shows and dinners. We even got into the habit of watching at least one movie every week after I found out Jax had never watched The Godfather.

Those moments alone with Jax had become my favorite part of the day. He managed to convince me to lower my guard and allow myself to feel safe, comfortable and truly adored by the man in my life. The only marks I obtained were the ones he made with his mouth, including a few handprints on my ass.

I knew my old scars would never fade properly, but Jax kissed and caressed each one like they were the most beautiful part of me. He never made me feel like I wasn't wanted or ugly nor made me believe he didn't care. He did care, in his own way and I had begun to see that.

The house arrest hadn't been for a punishment but for my safety. Apparently someone had leaked information about Jax and his new bride and that had caused a rise of new threats to the O'Hara's. His businesses were the first ones to get hit, which is why he spent a lot of time overseas mending the damages.

Next were his business partners, and when that didn't work they had threatened my life. Jax, looking ahead, made sure I wouldn't leave the security of his house and expose myself to an attack. And once that threat had been neutralized, he felt more comfortable letting me see the sun again.

Coming to the realization that everything Jax had done was executed with finesse and meticulous thought out intentions, made me swoon. No wonder he was nicknamed 'The Devil'. It seemed there was nothing, and I mean nothing, Jackal O'Hara couldn't do. I admired his ambition and dedication, and for the first time I wasn't afraid, I was happy.

"What are you thinking we should watch tonight?" I asked Jax while piling some pillows on the couch. Rolling up the sleeves, he leaned on the back of the couch, letting me admire his ink.

"You know well enough I don't know any movies."

"I still like to ask for your opinion. You want comedy, thriller, sci-fi?"

"Whatever you pick is fine."

"But I want you to enjoy it too."

"I enjoy watching you watching the movies." He leaned over and placed a kiss on my forehead. When he pulled back, his eyes held a strange softness one could mistake for a smile. "You aren't afraid of any gore or violence, but your whole body flinches from a jumpscare. You crunch up your nose at romantic scenes but huddle up closer during the steamy ones. But probably the best part is when you laugh so hard while holding your stomach it makes you snort."

"I don't snort."

"Oh yeah, you do snort. Like a little piggy." That deserved a smack on his chest which I delivered.

"Take that back."

"Hah. No."

"You're mean."

"I know. Now hurry up and pick the move while I get

some snacks for my little piggy."

I threw a well aimed pillow at his disappearing back but he managed to grab it mid air and throw it back at me. It hit me right in the face and I ended up on the floor with a thud. Scattering back to my feet, I finished building the nest, grabbed the remote and scrolled down to the horror section.

After a while Jax came back, all playfulness gone from his face as he tapped wildly on his phone. He hurried past the living room and towards the hidden cupboard which held his guns and other equipment. Jumping over the couch, I skidded across the floor to his side.

"What's wrong?"

Jax held the phone to his ear and looked at me while he waited for the call to pick up.

"It's my father. He's in trouble. I just got the message."

Knowing his intentions, I immediately grabbed his leather straps and holster, and proceeded to help him buckle it in. Next I unrolled his sleeves, buttoned up the cufflinks and checked the clips for the guns before handing them to him. He finished the call to his men and as he pocketed the phone, his lips were on mine. It was deep and rushed, but held so many emotions and unspoken words all at once.

"Petras will stay with you. Don't leave the house."

"Take care of yourself. Come back to me." I kissed him again as he stepped into the elevator.

We both knew it could be our last. We both knew the risks as we said our goodbyes. A pit fell into my stomach. The doors closed on the man I was not ready to lose but I refused to cry, blinking the tears away. His last word echoed in my head, just like many times before, when he vowed to return. *"Always."*

I paced in the living room fidgeting with my wedding ring, unable to focus on the movie blaring in the background, as my thoughts remained on Jax and his mission. It was not uncommon he had to fly out the door at a moment's notice to take care of his business. *So why am I feeling so anxious?*

Petras stationed himself by the front hall and I did my best trying to relax and ignore the bad feeling I had dwelling in my stomach.

When the end credits rolled over the screen, I couldn't remember anything I had just watched. Frustrated, I turned the tv off and cleared the nest. The house had fallen silent. The only noise came from the candy wrappers I bunched up in my fist to throw away. Crossing the hallway, I saw no sign of Petras anywhere.

Maybe I was paranoid, maybe it was the prickle in my gut or maybe it was the effects of the movie playing tricks on me, but I had an unnerving feeling in the back of my head I couldn't shake. I stepped further into the hallway trying to peer around the corner to see if he perhaps had gone into the kitchen for some reason.

The lights were off and everything seemed normal. Nothing out of the ordinary stood out to me. The counters were spotless and all the dishes had been put away after we finished our dinner. Even the coffee maker was set on a timer for tomorrow morning since the staff had a day off.

I turned, thinking I'd go upstairs to my room, but that's when I heard the safety of a gun being clicked off. Ducking to the hallway, a bang rang in my ears and a statue across the hall from me crumbled to the ground. Not looking back, I hurried to my feet. As I ran to the stairs, I dodged another bullet flying my way.

"Petras?! Where are you?" Flying up the stairs, I glanced back down to see many masked intruders rushing after me. *Fuck. Not good.* I counted at least six heads coming my way as I skipped the last flight of stairs to the top floor. "Petras! Help!"

Getting no response meant he was either dead or too far to hear me. My guess was on the first one. To my knowledge, I was on my own. Fear fueling my stride I ran to the end of the hallway and slammed the door shut. Jax's bedroom had a sturdy lock but I pushed a dresser in front of the door just in case they managed to break in. In that case I would have to defend myself.

Knowing Jax had a gun hidden in his nightstand, I rushed to grab it. It was a fine silver piece with carved details on the handle. I counted the rounds and cocked it just when I heard the first thump against the door.

The walls echoed with each forceful attempt at the door. They took a few shots but didn't even make a dent in it. For a second I felt the slightest glee at my husband for thinking ahead by reinforcing the doors.

The shouts that carried through the walls were muffled but I could guess they were making threats to my life. I was on borrowed time. It wouldn't take them long to figure a way to either break the door, which meant I would be cornered and outnumbered. I had to think fast.

First I needed to get my phone. I had left it in my room on a charger and getting it meant I could call for backup. Tying my hair out of my face, I did a quick scan around the room forming the plan. Initially I thought I'd somehow spiderman my way on the outer wall to my bedroom, but when inspecting the glass, I spotted a vent in the corner. A much less daredevil kind of option.

The banging at the door hadn't stopped and the yelling

only seemed to increase in volume as the minutes ticked by. I removed my belt and used the buckle to unscrew the grate. The opening was small but with hope I'd be able to squeeze in by contorting my body. After the first failed attempt, I quickly stripped off a few layers of clothing to make myself as narrow as possible to then try again. I was left in nothing but a bra, a thin top and boyshorts.

This time I managed to slide into the vent more easily. It was dark and dusty but I could see the light at the end of the tunnel. My bedroom was not too far from his. I began to crawl, slowly inching my way towards the light and prayed there would not be any roaches on the way.

The sounds of the intruders faded but I could still hear them rummaging around the house. Things were being bashed, furniture turned over and glass was smashed for no reason but to intimidate me. I could only imagine all the destruction Jax would return home to. His beautiful pristine home, completely eviscerated and his wife probably dead, if I didn't find a way to escape or defeat the invaders.

The dust creeped up my nose and I had to suppress a sneeze and avoid alerting the crooks to my location. I didn't want them to know I had managed to leave the room they were so desperate to get into. I held my breath passing other vent openings, dragging my body deeper into the tunnel and finally saw the metal grate leading into my room.

It was screwed shut just like the one I had gotten in from. *Shit.* My fingers could barely fit through the iron bars and there was no way I could unscrew it from this side. Thinking, I would have to break it open and risk causing some noise, scared me. But I had to try.

It didn't take long till another bang rattled through the

house. I timed hitting the grate to the same rhythm as the intruders were still banging at Jax's bedroom door. Again and again I put my fist and palm against the metal, hissing through the pain from each blow. The hinge cracked and bent, allowing me to push the grate aside and pull myself out of the vent.

I rushed to my phone, quickly dialed and held it to my ear, tiptoeing to the bathroom looking for bandages. Nothing but the empty tone sounded back at me. No answer. *Double shit.* I tried Jax's number a few more times with no results. Calling the police was not an option. *I can't risk revealing Jax's private residence to the force. Bet they would have a field day going through this place.* I was no rat. Not even when my life depended on it. This much I knew growing up as the daughter of bratva.

I put the phone next to the gun on the floor and wrapped my knuckles quickly and quietly, while listening to the commotion happening just on the other side of the wall. *Okay, new plan. Think, Katy, think.* I bit my lip and stilled my breath, willing my racing heart to calm down. Now was not the time to panic. If I could not get help to come to me I would have to go to them. I would have to find my way to Jax, wherever he was. *Forgive me. I have to leave the penthouse.*

Phone and gun in hand, I tiptoed to the door. I was not going to crawl my way through the entire house. But I was not going to walk in front of the swarming enemies either. One thing about the house was that it was always spotless. Louisa was very matriculate about keeping the mess out of sight, hence there was a utility closet on every floor and a laundry chute leading to the laundry room on the bottom. Laundry room was next to the kitchen, and my way out.

Cracking the door open I peeked out and saw the mob still hammering at the door. They had picked up a table using it like a ram but making little progress breaking down the door. *Good luck,* I thought sarcastically, as I slipped out to the hallway and quickly snuck my way towards the closet.

It was no bigger than a powder room but held all the essentials for a spotless house. Rows and rows of bottles filled with different cleaning liquids sat neatly on the shelves, a pair of gloves hung on a hook and a cluster of mops lay resting against the wall. I whipped open the hatch to peer down to the seemingly endless pit. This was not going to be easy.

Shoving the phone and the gun under my waistband, I threw my legs over the edge and wedged my body between the narrow walls. Another tight journey, only this time it was vertical. One wrong move and I would plunge to a certain death. *Not terrifying in the least.*

I swiped the sweat from my hands and began the dangerous climb down the chute. The walls were smooth and made gripping on to them almost impossible. I had to keep my body constantly pressed against opposing walls to remain suspended in the limited space.

The air quality in the chute wasn't the best either. After what felt like an hour inching my way down in the tube I was panting and sweating profusely. It became increasingly more laboursome to hold my body weight with just the tension of my arms and legs. *I should have spent more time in the home gym.* I cursed at myself, silently vowing to do more training if I survived tonight. *That's if I survive. Don't get ahead of yourself, Katy.*

Soap fragrant air was my first fresh lungfull I took as I made the last jump into the basket below the chute. My ankles were throbbing and every muscle in my body was filled with acid but at least I was alive, for now. I stilled and listened to the sounds of the house. Nothing new but the steady thumping and shouting coming from above. *Fuck these assholes.*

Deeming the kitchen empty from the intruders, I stepped out of the laundry room only to trip on something laying across the floor. I planted face first on the ground, almost breaking my nose. I bit my tongue so as not to scream but it hurt like a motherfuck. Rolling around I saw a body, bloodied and tied up, tucked behind the counter.

"Holy fucking shit. Petras?" I whispered, testing for pulse. *Alive. Good.* I spent a good minute shaking him awake and listening to the sounds coming from upstairs. His eyes fluttered open and I moved a finger to my lips, I motioned him to roll over so I could untie him. "What the fuck happened?"

"I got knocked out. I don't know who or how they got into the house."

"We've got to get out of here. Can you drive?"

"Yes, mam."

I glanced around to make sure it was safe to stand before getting off the floor. The sounds from upstairs had gone quiet. "Okay, we've got to hurry."

"On a second though, I think you should drive."

"What-" I looked down and saw that his entire white shirt was drenched in blood. He doubled down and pressed a hand to his side. *'Mother fuckers'* was the only thing I could make out from his muffled grunts. Thinking on my feet, I grabbed a tea towel off the hook and pressed it against his wound. It was a miracle he hadn't already bled to death. "Easy there. I've got you. Lean on me."

His steps staggered, but with one arm over my shoulder and my arm going around his waist, I was able to hold his bodyweight and lead us towards the door. He was heavy but I wasn't about to leave him behind. One foot in front of the other, I practically carried him to the elevator.

"Hey! Over there!" I heard a second before the guns began to sing.

The elevator dinged, I pushed Petras into the cabin and pulled out the gun to return fire. Bullets went off flying, hitting the walls, the metal around the elevator and a few of them even made it into the cabin. Hunching behind the narrow side panel for cover, I blindly aimed at the other shooters.

"She's escaping. Get her!"

I smashed the button for the garage and held them off till it finally closed. The pit in my stomach flipped as the elevator jumped into motion, descending rapidly. *89... 88... 87...* Petras was groaning on the ground, bleeding through the towel. *62... 61... 60...* My heart was pounding in my head and I was sure I had a few too many close calls from that fight. *37... 36... 35...* The floors ticked down as I checked the clip. It was not enough for another fight.

"Keys?"

"P-pocket." Crouching next to him I rummaged around his jacket till I found the small black puck with a car logo on it. *14... 13... 12...* I checked the wound under the towel. It didn't look good. Putting pressure on it I attempted to get him up but it proved to be more difficult than before. "L-leave me. Just g-go."

"I'm not fucking leaving you here to die."

The door dinged again and the freezing air from the

garage flooded the cabin. My nipples hardened in an instant and my skin was crawling with goose bumps. Not wasting any time I began dragging him out of the elevator. With the puck still in my hand, I pressed the 'unlock' button and a vehicle on the other end of the garage not too far from the exit blinked.

"Just hang in there. Almost there."

Somehow I endured the coldness nipping at my bare skin as I dragged Petras through the entire parking garage to the car. Heaving, I pulled his body up and pushed him to the back seat. His agonizing cries let me know he was still alive, barely. The guy was a champ. I slammed the door shut just as I heard approaching footsteps coming from the fire escape stairwell.

I ducked behind cover in time for the first bullets to fly over my head and into the adjacent vehicles, popping their tires and windows. Jumping to the driver's side, I shoved the key into the ignition and made the car roar to life. I quickly pulled the car out of the square and pressed my foot on the pedal, skidding the tires on the asphalt while bullets chased after our dust.

I did a momentary victory dance in my head while keeping my eyes on the road. Dialing Jax's number again, I hoped he would answer this time. Traffic was light which, lucky for me, made it easy to maneuver between the other cars. Ignoring all the red lights, I zoomed past so many crossings I was surprised I hadn't crashed into anything yet. *C'mon, pick up.*

Even though the roads were mostly clear of snow, the ice caused the car to drift every time I made a turn. My heart rate was through the roof, holding a death grip on the steering wheel while driving to another dreadful corner. Shooting a glance at the rear view mirror, all I saw was black vehicles racing towards us. *Shit, shit, shit.* I shifted the car into a higher gear and pressed on the pedal even harder.

Petras kept wheezing, probably bleeding all over the black leather seat. A loud bang rang in my ears as the back window collapsed and the cold air rushed into the vehicle. Bullets rained on us despite my best efforts to sway on the road trying to dodge them. A litany of curse words in my native tongue left my lips as I turned around to return fire. I shot over my shoulder, tagged one of their tires and kept shooting till the clip was empty.

As expected, the gunshots and the reckless driving quickly attracted the attention of the law enforcement. The sirens blare echoed throughout the city.

Pick up your stupid phone. Please.

Red and blue flashed before my eyes, forcing me to make a U-turn. The car spinned on its axis a couple of times, burning a ring at the crossing. Police vehicles to my left and black suv's to my right, I pulled the car in reverse, revved the engine and hurled down a free street, leaving them in dust.

Clutching the gears, I pushed the car to its limit, driving with no end in sight. Another red light. I almost hit a car, barely missing the front bumper by swaying to the right and crashing into the back of another one instead. The metal groaned, leaving behind a long tiger stripe of absent paint on both of our vehicles as I rushed to get out of the scene. *Sorry.* I didn't even have time to look back if they were okay.

I kept calling Jax. No answer. I dialed again, and again and again. Nothing. The dial tone was the only thing I got back from the desperate calling. *Hopeless.* The situation was hopeless, and I feared it would end only one way.

"Jesus fucking christ answer the fucking phone. I need you!"

Chapter 8

Meanwhile on the other side of the city.

A fresh layer of snow fell, covering the road I was on. The line of black SUV's stood dormant by the side of the road, hidden away from the industrial compound in the distance, waiting for my arrival. In the distance, stood an old factory warehouse. The site was abandoned, or maybe they wanted us to believe it to be that way. We were outside of any known clan territory, which made the location unpredictable.

As I stepped out of my car and fetched a cigarette out of my pocket, one of my guards offered me the flame of his lighter. With the first inhale, I could feel the smoke filling my lungs and numbing my nerves.

"Was the drive here difficult?"

"Cut the crap, Quentin. What's the status?"

"We've circled the area and there are no civilians in a two mile radius. They have guards at the gate to the north and west, and sout-east is only accessible by the river. It's not frozen solid so that could be an angel. Felix is still trying to find security footage but these old buildings rarely have anything high tech if I'm perfectly honest."

"Any word from the inside?"

"None since the first call and we lost contact with the scouting team ten minutes ago."

"Fuck. So we're going in blind?"

"I don't know-"

"Then find me someone who does!"

"Yes, boss."

Idiot. Watching him scurry off to gather more intel, I made a mental note to have him moved to desk duties till the foreseeable future. I couldn't afford to have a weak link on the field, but for now I let it slide. Half of my men were on other duties across the seas so I had summoned any able body I could on such short notice.

"Speak."

Felix didn't even lift his gaze off the laptop he was working on as I climbed to the back of the van. Monitors, tablets and other equipment lined the walls. The air was filled with a static buzz.

"Working on it."

"You gotta give me something."

"Just gimmi a minute." The tapping intensified as he stared at the monitor.

While waiting, I scrolled through my phone to peek into the home security system. Katy was still in the living room watching the movie. I wasn't particularly thrilled having to leave her alone, but I was pleased she didn't make a fuss about it either. She understood. She knew our lifestyle and the risks and consequences that came with it. Any other regular woman would have thrown a fit for abandoning her on our date night. But not Katy, and that's what I liked about her.

"Boss? I've got something."

"Show me."

A fuzzy black and white live image flashed on the screen. The warehouse was dark with only a few spotlights from parked cars illuminating a group of people huddled in a circle with their guns ready. Though the image wasn't clear, I could still recognize the silhouette of my father in the middle. Nobody else would be wearing that ridiculous fedora.

"What the hell are they waiting for? Are they expecting us to just waltz in there guns blazing? Zoom in on that."

"Sorry. This is the best I got. The camera is ancient. I was lucky to even pull this feed."

"Alright. Keep an eye on it. Find out everything you can in the meantime. I want to know exactly who we are dealing with."

"You got it, boos. Imma need radio silence to operate this in these conditions. The signal can only handle so much."

I nodded and proceeded to give a briefing to the other men. Our mission was to rescue my father and any other members still alive with as little casualties as possible. I wasn't opposed to simply gunning the place down, but I couldn't risk my father getting injured in the process.

We switched off our phones, screwed on the silencers and started moving towards the compound, using the high snow banks as cover. Once we reached the fence, the wire was cut to create a hole for us to crawl through and proceed closer to the warehouse.

My breath created a cloud of vapors in the air as I inspected the exterior of the building. The concrete was cracked in various places, many windows had shattered over time and the walls were heavily tagged with spray paint. It was clear that the property had been neglected for a long time, which made it the perfect cover for illegal activities.

Approaching cautiously, we scaled the side of the building and entered through the fire escape on the second floor. The door swung open to a pitch black hallway, filled with eerie and hollow sounds. Frost had laid a glittering blanket over the filthy grime covered floor that crunched under my feet as I moved in slowly.

Motioning to the men to split up, I carried on further into the building, lightening my steps. I had instructed my men to secure our position before making a move on the targets. I was surprised they didn't have anyone patrolling the offices in the upper floors as I found them empty.

Making my way down a set of stairs, I found myself on the ground floor. The space was crowded with rows and rows of shelves, though not entirely empty, the contents left behind had a significant amount of wear and tear. Crouching down behind one tall box, the smell of mold and petrol made my eyes water in the narrow space.

Holding my breath, I inched my way further into the warehouse, staying close to the wall as possible and blending in with the shadows. The small movements above me let me know my men were making their way into their position on the railings. The darkness swallowed them entirely; you wouldn't be able to see them unless you were looking directly at them.

A guard stood by the door, facing away from me, unknowing he, just like his compatriots, would be taking their last breaths tonight. Another guard shuffled in place on the other side of the shelves. It was over in a blink of an eye. I pounced from my hiding spot, tackled the first guard and silently rang his neck, silencing him forever just as Miko did the same to the other one. He laid the guy down gently avoiding the sound his limp body would have made hitting the ground.

We crept further, taking out the roaming guards one by one without raising the alarm. It was easy. Almost too easy. None of them had any insignias on their clothing, no distinguishable tattoos or other marks that would indicate to their clan. As if all of them were nameless mercenaries, hired by someone to act like initiated crew members. My suspicions grew as the last one that I killed didn't even have their identification in their pockets. Something wasn't right.

"Listen buddy, I'm tired of waitin' around." A murmur broke the deafening silence once I settled behind the parked cars. The speaker's silhouette remained dark and unrecognizable even from this close proximity. Quietly observing, I let my eyes adjust to the spotlights. "I don't think anyone's coming."

"Oh they're coming. I made sure of it." Another man spoke, keeping their voice low, almost inaudible beyond their circle of cronies. The irritation in their voice was clear though.

"Tis' better be worth it, man."

As on que, I saw my men closing in on the circle, pistols in hand. Like a well orchestrated symphony, all acted at once and pressed the barrels at the back of their heads as I stepped into the light. With a quick glance, I had made the unnerving discovery that the man in the fedora was not in fact my father, but someone else entirely. Someone who resembled my father almost too well to be a coincidence. My pistol rose to greet the imposter.

"You have exactly two minutes to explain yourself."

"Ah, Mr. O'Hara. So glad you could join us."

"You already know my name, how bout you tell me yours."

"Lee MacCoy." He smiled and extended his hand, being obnoxiously casual, like we were already old friends. My hand did not waver, keeping him staring at the barrel of my gun. "A pleasure to meet your acquaintance."

"Minute forty-five. The feeling is not mutual. Where is my father?"

"Where's the rush? We're all gents here rite'?"

"Answer the fucking question or I'll start dropping bodies."

"Such hostilities. Perhaps we could-"

Bang! The first body dropped as a result of one of my men delivering a silenced bullet to the head. MacCoy didn't even flinch but the disgusting smile fell and he stopped talking immediately.

"I wasn't kidding, so stop the theatrics and answer the goddamn question."

"Fine. Seems like you are all work and no play." He spread his arms in mock surrender. "Mr. O'Hara *the senior* is not here."

"Obviously." I gritted my teeth, finger itching on the trigger.

"But he was never here in the first place. So, you needn't be so feisty. This isn't necessary-"

Bang! Another body hit the ground with a thud. MacCoy held his gaze, the bright lights reflecting in the continuously irritating stare he had squared on me, alarmingly unblinking. His demeanor was getting more fidgety, more unstable as the seconds ticked by.

"I decide what's necessary. One minute left."

"I told you I-" *Bang!* My patience had run its course and I snapped.

Placing a bullet neatly in his knee socket, he fell to his side, huffing and roaring out of pain. I knew exactly where to aim, high enough to render him immobile but low enough to avoid the major artery, lest he bleed to death before I had my answers.

"Motherfucker!"

"Unless the next words out of your mouth aren't 'Mr. O'Hara is located in *this* address' I'm going to put a bullet in your shoulder."

"Urgh, you son of a-"

Bang! I was getting really tired of this whole ordeal. Scolding myself for not going with my initial thought of just gunning them down, as it would have saved me a ton of time with the same result. I still had no clarity on why I had been summoned here in the first place.

"Next one goes to your head so answer quickly. Where is my father?"

"A-alrite' alrite' calm down." His breathing came out in shallow rasps as he rolled on the ground, all playfulness stripped away.

The men that had accompanied him made no move in attempts to retaliate. They stood rigid, frozen to their spot, waiting for the inevitable. MacCoy spat out blood, staining the ground between my feet.

"H-he's not here. Wait wait wait don't shoot!" He spat as I pressed my gun to his temple. "I mean we don't have him. It was just a lure. A decoy to get you out of the house. I swear. That's all."

"The house?" *What the fuck did they want with my house?* Most of my valuables were secured in various vaults and safety deposits. Everything in my house was either insured or guarded by an advanced security system, not to mention my entire staff was highly trained against anything threatening my property. There was nothing they could be stupid enough to even attempt stealing. *Unless.*

Something in me stirred, making my stomach flip and bile to rise to my throat. *Katy.* She was alone, except for Petras, who I had ordered to not let her out of his sight. I told her to stay in the house. She was safe there. *Wasn't she?*

I needed more answers but there was no time to question him. The need to know she was safe had me spinning on my heels. Digging my phone out of my pocket, I signaled to my men to finish the job. The loud thuds echoed in the warehouse, leaving only one whimpering soul, bleeding and suffering on the ground. I would have my fun later, but first I needed to get a hold of Katy. I needed to know she was okay and that nothing had aspired during my absence.

Turning on the phone seemed to take ages, and when it finally did, my heart deflated. At least a dozen missed calls, the first time stamped a mere minute after I switched off my phone. Inwardly I cursed at myself. If only I hadn't been so hasty to get to my father. If only I hadn't left her alone. If only I hadn't switched off my phone.

An unnerving chill ran down my spine when the phone rang again. My heartbeat spiked as I swiped the screen and pressed the phone to my ear. A mixture of sounds flooded through. First it was the beeping of car horns, then police sirens, gunshots and finally a small breathy sob calling out to me.

"Jax?"

"Katy?"

"*Oh my god, Jax! Finally! Where the fuck have you been?*

I've tried to call you like a million times."

"What's going on? Where are you? Sounds like-"

"Like a fucking mess. I need help. Petras is going to die. I don't-" A sickening sound of metal being crushed and the choir of horns blasted through the phone speaker. I heard the wheels screeching and the engine roar, while Katy spat out every Russian curse word she knew. *"Ah. Shit!"*

"Where are you?"

"Umh, I- hold on. I don't know."

"Katy, I can't help you if I don't know where you are. Please. Try."

"Ahh. Move, dumbass! Sorry, I'm fine. Maybe."

"Katy!" My feet moved on their own, faster than ever before. I could feel the stress and anxiety in her voice. The sheer panic got my pulse to rise to a dangerous level. She was not safe.

"Okay, wait-" The gunshots and the sirens were competing to see which one was the loudest, deafening some of her cries as she made the car hurl once again. *"I think I'm close to the pasta place you took me. Yes, yes. I see the sign. Oh fuck, the cops have the road blocked."*

"Take the next left if you can." I instructed. I knew exactly where she was. An image of her smiling across from me in the candle lit room flashed before my eyes, but it vanished when I heard her groan. I was not far from her. "You need to head to the west to get across the bridge."

"Across the bridge?" Stepping outside I could hear the distant blaring of the sirens carrying over the river. Though the night was murky, the flashing of red and blue against the sky was clear, even from this far away.

"Yes. I'm coming to you. Just hang on a little longer." I picked up the pace and flagged down the men standing by the rendezvous point. Needn't to explain with more than a few words, they climbed in one of the vehicles while I jumped in mine and skidded away from the site.

"I don't think- Holy shit! Ah! Jax!"

I didn't know what was more terrifying; hearing the chaos echo in the distance knowing she was part of the chase or to witness the despair in Katy's voice as she raced through the city. The road banked to the right and I gripped on to the steering wheel so hard I thought I might break it.

"It's okay. You've got this." The car whined in protest when I forced it into a higher gear, speeding towards the side of the river where the bridge ended.

"Oh I see the bridge."

I could almost see her. Stopping at the docks, I scanned the bridge above for any sight of her. The speeding black dot was certainly her, swaying through traffic, barely avoiding the collisions. The police cruisers stood unmoving, barricading the exit.

"Son of a- It's blocked. They've got me. I don't know what to do?"

"Drive off the bridge."

"Are you insane?"

"Do it now, Katy! You've got to trust me." The dot got closer and closer to the blockade, barreling towards them at full speed. She was going to crash no matter what. "Now!"

"Shit, shit, shit."

The vehicle hit the barrier, breaking it on impact and plummeted to the river, sinking to the depths below.

Chapter 9

Feeling a mixture of relief and fury when Jax finally answered his phone was almost too overwhelming. First I felt like I wanted to scream at him for not being there when I needed him. He was supposed to protect me and keep me safe. I knew the risks and expected something like this would happen but I still hoped that it wouldn't and I'd be okay. I was outraged, furious to the point I wanted to kill him for leaving me alone.

Rage fueled by my fear was boiling inside me, but as soon as I heard his voice, that anger melted away. Hope surged through my body, hammering my heart to a different beat. If I wasn't currently being chased by murderous psychos and the cops, I might have been jumping for joy.

The end of the bridge was approaching faster than I would have liked. I gasped, weaving through the other cars, avoiding getting hit by the bullets as they whizzed by. One glance out of the windshield revealed the end of the line for me. The police had set up a barricade and I could hear them shouting orders through a megaphone for me to stop; but the only thing I could hear was Jax's voice commanding me even louder.

"Are you insane?"

"Do it now, Katy! You've got to trust me. Now!"

"Shit, shit, shit." I screamed, rotating the wheel hard right and driving nose first into the railing of the bridge. Metal on metal screeched and groaned as the barrier gave out from the shear force of the car leaping into the void. The airbags finally inflated, the car nose dipped and then we were in free fall.

The horror that stared back at me was beyond my ability to withhold the strangled wail that tore from my throat. Dark waters waited below to welcome us to its cold embrace. I might as well have been staring at the open mouth of a monster. The sight of it had fear washing over me, turning my blood into ice and stopping my heart altogether. It was a precursor to what was to come. The surface broke, splitting and splashing the water around the vehicle, swallowing us in a whirlpool to the depths.

The cockpit filled with freezing cold water, surging up my legs and chilling me to the core. I had to fight hard not to let the panic take over me, as I crawled to the backseat, grabbed the hold of unconscious Petras and attempted to pull him out of the car before we sank completely. He was heavy, limp and unmovable and I was unsure if he was even still alive. I didn't have time to check. Unfortunately I was unsuccessful and the water rushed in within seconds, taking us in its icy hold.

Forcefully I drew in a harsh breath just as my head dipped under the surface. My skin tingled and burned, every muscle in my body convulsed and my head started to throb, fighting the shock. Petras' body floated weightlessly and I was finally able to tug him out of the cabin. Glass scraped and tore what was left of my flimsy top, rendering it all but scraps clinging to my body. Not that it mattered. I was minutes away from hypothermia and seconds away from drowning. A shredded item of clothing was the least of my worries.

Petras hung on my arm as I peddled towards what I hoped was the surface, since everything around me was pitch black. My body was becoming numb, my lungs screamed for air and my head felt like there was a stake pierced through it. I pushed past the discomfort and kicked with what little energy I still had.

This is it, I thought, *this is how I die. From all the scenarios I had thought out, all the threats I've received for my life, all the dangers that had tested my surviving skills, this was the way I was going to die?*

My vision blurred and I stopped struggling, no longer caring for the blistering cold invading my body. The river was calm, a deafening silence falling over me and there was all but nothingness left.

Badump. My heartbeat was but a tired drum, echoing somewhere, hollow and weak, far from the hammering thunder it had been before. *Badump.* Another beat, slower and quiet, like the melody it once sang now lost and forgotten, and all that remained was barely a whisper. *Badump.* One last time, the pulse gave a gentle throb, setting free its final cadence as it finally stilled and I spirited away.

Badump.

A shocking gasp ripped through my lungs. My body jolted upwards, turning on its side and coughing up whatever it was stuck in my throat. I felt the struggling rasps of my breathing, as I drew in heavy lungfulls, shivering and shaking uncontrollably with every intake. Incoherent mumbling resonated above me but I couldn't quite understand it, like it was muffled and distorted, or in another language. Either way I wasn't able to decipher it and it made me frustrated and tired.

A splitting headache forced me to reach for my temples but my hands wouldn't move. In fact nothing of me was moving voluntarily. I attempted to move my arms to feel my *anything* but they remained still on my lap. Seemingly immobile, I focused all my capacity to use my other senses, but it felt as if I had none. I couldn't smell, taste or feel anything. My lids were heavy and my hearing had yet returned, which only added to the annoyance.

"Stay with me, stay with me, Katy. Don't you dare die on me. Don't you fucking dare."

What is he saying? Slayning? What's slayning? Who's Kaygy? No, who is he? I wracked my brain but could not recognize the voice. *Hey, buddy, I don't know you. Can you like step away from me? Or at least tell me what is daining?*

"I've got you. Fuck." The voice got louder, I assumed to talk to someone else, but I couldn't be certain. He might have just been yelling at me too. If only I could have understood what he was saying I wouldn't have been so clueless. "Can't you go any faster?! Just hurry."

Uuh okay. Why is everything wobbling? Stop rocking the damn boat. Imma be sick. If there was one thing I didn't need to come back to me, was feeling nauseous, even though there was nothing left in my stomach. *Why aren't you listening? I'm talking to you. Aren't I? Hello?*

"Please, Katy. Open your eyes. Please. I'll never forgive myself if-"

Oh. Why do you sound so sad? What's wrong? Hey, sir. Would you mind telling em.. What's going on, please - sorry?

Umm.

"Just hang on for a little longer. Okay? I'm sorry, Katy. I'm so fucking sorry. Please. You have to get through this. Please. You will get through this. You've got to survive. Just keep fighting, okay? Fight for me. For us."

The rest of the conversation faded away and I let my mind go blank.

Next time I regained my consciousness, I felt my body tingling, like something was pricking and stabbing me with tiny needles. Like blistering heat going on a rampage and reaching every corner of my body. I didn't like it at all. Not for one bit. The horace sound that left my throat was not my own. I groaned, willing my body to respond in any other way but I seemed to ragdoll on something. I was limp like a wet noodle.

"Katy? You're awake. Thank fuck. I thought-" The voice of the man was familiar, friendly, soothing even. He spoke in a low soft tone with a hint of panic, and though I didn't know why, I could feel my heart constrict. This man sounded worried and was still very close to me, maybe even touching me. I couldn't tell. The burning sensation was unbearable, scorching my skin, making it almost impossible to focus on anything else.

"Hot." I mumbled, surprised at the weak squeak it turned out to be.

"I promise you it's not hot."

Bull shit. My skin was practically burning off. Whatever he was doing didn't feel right and hurt like a motherfucker. I wanted to slap him, but my arms refused to move. *This is ridiculous.*

"You just might feel like it is. Your body has been through a shock."

"Hurts." Another pathetic whimper came out of my

91

mouth. My own voice felt so foreign to me. Something or someone was pressing on my back. Even when I tried to wiggle away from it, I found myself being pulled back.

"I know, Katy. I'm sorry. Just bear with me. I've got you. I have to do this. You'll feel better soon. I promise."

I could not bring myself to care what they were saying or doing, I just wanted the burning pain to end, so I hung my head and drifted off to sleep again.

When I woke up the third time, the blistering heat was gone but the tingling sensation still remained. Slowly, I mentally tested all my limbs, that I still had them and that they were working. I was wrapped up in something like a cocoon and based on the sway of my legs, I guessed I was being carried. Wiggling my toes I determined them all there and did the same with my fingers, rejoicing that the numbness was slowly receding. Jolts of electricity shot from my fingertips to my spine and up the back of my head, sparking every nerve ending to awake anew.

I let out a shocked gasp and flashed open my eyes, which I regretted immediately. A bright light beaming down at me had me squinting at my carrier. With a groan, I squirmed but only ended up being held on tighter, almost to the point where I struggled to breathe. Peering up, I saw the tight jaw of a man. His hair was messy and sticking out of place as if he had run fingers through it a lot. I reached up from my bindings and touched it, finding it slightly damp. The man's eyes dropped down to meet my gaze.

"Hey?" I tried, testing out my voice again that still sounded raspy and weak. It was a mere whisper, but he heard it all the same. A crease formed between his brows and I bit my lip not knowing the reason for his worry. Finally my mind reeled and I was able to recognize him.

"Jackal?"

"Almost there. How're you feeling?"

"Umh, I don't know. What's going on? What happened?"

"Do you remember anything?"

"I remember-" Closing my eyes, I thought back, hard, racking my brain for the fragments of my memories.

Images flashed before my eyes, events I could recall and faces I was familiar with, and some I was unfamiliar with; faces with masks. A shiver ran down my spine, fear washing over me as the memories flickered into view, each more clear than the next. The images were moving so fast it was hard to keep up, like my brian was working overtime trying to place everything that had happened back in the timeline.

There was blood and glass everywhere, the smell of gunpowder and gasoline still fresh in my mind and my ears were still ringing from the wailing of police sirens. And then I remembered the water. And the cold. And-

"Oh my god. Petras? Is he-?"

"The men fished him out of the river too. He was unconscious, but miraculously there was a pulse. He is in a coma. It's a miracle if he survives. Would be a shame to lose a good guy like him." He lowered me onto a bed and continued to pull out the covers, placing the blankets on top of me and wrapping me up like a breakfast burrito. "I don't want you to think about that right now. You should focus on yourself. The doctor is on his way."

"What happened? After the crash I mean."

He grimaced and I reached out to him, but he pushed my hands back inside the blankets.

"Please. I want to know."

He sat on the edge of the bed, leaned his elbows on his

knees and sighed. In the dim light I finally got to really *see* him. Worry weighed heavy on his shoulders. I couldn't recall ever seeing him like this. Not once. He always wore the same expression, like he was unaffected by the things happening around him. The perfect poker face. In this fleeting moment, he seemed bothered, hurt even, and my heart ached to comfort him.

"Where you went under, it wasn't too far from the shore. I was already on the pier when you crashed through the barricade, however I was not expecting the car to sink so fast. And when I didn't see you come up, I lost it."

"I'm sorry."

"What for?"

"For-" I wasn't sure what exactly but I felt like I needed to say something. "-bothering you?"

"Fuck, Katy. It's a little late for that." He let out a sigh raking his hands through his hair once more. "The moment I saw you, even before I knew who you were, I knew you would be trouble. I knew a pretty girl that looked like sin incarnate would end up costing me more than I was ready to bargain for. And yet I didn't fight it when my father presented you as my bride, because devil be damned I wanted you all the same."

My body numb and void of energy, I shuddered from his confession. I couldn't cry even if I wanted to, feeling overwhelmed by his words and only a pitiful whimper was what left my lips in response.

He turned to face me and placed a kiss on my forehead, before leaning on it and holding me tight in his arms. My heart was about to burst.

"Don't think for a second that you are a bother. You are my wife, my responsibility and I-" His voice broke above me as his body trembled. "-I've failed you. I couldn't protect you. I'm sorry. I'm so fucking sorry, Katy. I'm sorry-"

Wiggling my arms free from the bundle, I reached around his neck and pulled him onto me tighter, sealing him in my embrace as he tightened his grip around me, too. His weight was crushing and seized my breath but I didn't care. I needed him closer. I choked out a cry as I felt his lips in the nape of my neck, raining soft kisses on my exposed skin.

Far too soon, he lifted himself off me when a knock sounded off somewhere in the room. I hadn't even paid attention to where we were till he got off the bed to answer the door. The unfamiliar room was small with narrow windows, gray wallpaper and furniture adorned with light wood trims.

Jax pulled out his gun on instinct and marched to the door. A man in a trench coat didn't even flinch when the barrel was aimed at his head. With a nod, Jax put his gun down and the man pushed past him, rushed to the bedside and put his medical bag on the nightstand. He proceeded to shed his outer layers, and pulled on some white latex gloves before approaching me.

"I came as fast as I could. On the phone you said she drowned. This is not a place to treat a patient. I still think she should go to the hospital."

"No, we can't risk it. I don't know who is involved. They might have set up an ambush at nearby hospitals and emergency rooms. She will stay here."

"Fine. I'll do what I can with what I got. May I?" He asked, pressing the glasses further on his crooked nose. I nodded and he began his examination.

An oxygen mask was pulled over my face and he took

my vitals, including blood pressure and drew some blood. Jax stayed by my side the entire time and for once he was not on his phone. His hand rested on mine rubbing small circles on it and occasionally he placed a kiss on my knuckles. My eyes were droopy again and I could barely keep up with everything that the doctor was doing. I laid my head on the pillow as the small pads were being attached to my skin and the covers pulled over me.

"Rest, Katy."

"But..."

"Hush, it's okay. Just focus on getting better. I'll take care of everything. I promise."

The room faded away and I believe I mumbled a weak 'okay' as a response before sleep overtook me once more.

Chapter 10

During my recovery I was told this was one of the safe houses scattered around the city, only one of the many all over the country that Jax owned. For the first few days I stayed in bed, in a drip and under the mask, mostly sleeping and drugged up. *Could have been more than a few days, couldn't tell.* The doctor stayed in the house just in case I developed any complications.

The house was fully stocked in case someone had to stay in hiding for a long period of time. Each bedroom had a wardrobe full of both men's and women's clothing. In case of emergencies, which was often, they had a plentiful stack of medical supplies. And then there was the kitchen which was my favorite room of the house. It wasn't anything special but was stocked regularly and made sure it had plenty of long lasting food, canned goods and other groceries stored for a rainy day.

Most of the days I spent in silence, wondering what was happening back in the city. Even with dozens of guards in the house, I felt slightly lonely. Jax had stayed away from the house and because all communication had been cut off due to the security breach, I had no way of contacting him. Worry and a sour feeling in my gut was a constant companion as the days dragged on. My anxiety was eased only by the little nuggets of information I managed to gather from the guards regarding the situation outside the walls of my sanctuary.

One evening, just as I was settling in bed for the night, I heard a commotion from outside. The sounds of multiple people stomping and shouting carried to my ears. Startled, I rushed to the door, grabbing the knife I had for protection. The guard standing in the hallway was blocking the doorway with his gun drawn.

"Madam, stay inside."

"Tony? What's happening?"

"Hold on, I'll check." He rushed to the top of the stairs to peer down. The noise was louder now and I could feel the chaos happening below. "It's the boss. He's back and-"

I didn't need to hear anything more. Rushing past him, I skipped the steps two at a time and reached the bottom in a matter of seconds, my heart leaping in my chest. The scene taking place had me halting my steps. At least a dozen men in different states of hurt were being carried inside and laid down on any available surface. The doctor that had treated me was already in full motion, assessing the situation. The cries and grunts of agony filled the air along with the smell of blood and sweat.

"Holy shit, what happened?"

"Ambush." Jax said, as he appeared next to me, and scooped me up rushing back upstairs. I landed on his shoulder with an umph. His grip around my thighs was bruising but I didn't dare to complain. He had returned.

As soon as my feet hit the floor of the bedroom, his

mouth was on me. His arms remained tightly around my back, pulling me flush against his body as his lips branded my skin. His touch was brutal, so full of raw emotions I could not decipher. Responding to his feverish touch, I sank my fingers in his hair and tugged at the roots, deepening the kiss.

His mouth was everywhere. I felt his teeth scrape the sensitive skin on my neck, then at my shoulder, till he nibbled his way back to my jaw. Gasping for air and moaning, I captured his lips again, drunk on the taste of him on my tongue.

My fingers roamed over his muscular shoulders and down his chest and abs, digging under his shirt-

What the fuck?

Breaking the kiss, I pulled out my fingers and found them stained red, wet from blood.

"Jax, you're bleeding."

"It's fine." He growled, tugging me back against his chest and kissing me again. With great effort I managed to squirm out of his grasp and push him at arm's length.

"No it's not!"

"Don't worry about it. Come here-"

"No. Jax, please. Let me take a look at you."

I ignored his protest and pulled his shirt till the thread holding the buttons ripped and sent them flying across the room. His chest was marvelous, an absolute work of art. I had yet to discover the meaning behind all of his tattoos. My fingers trailed his abs down to the side of his bloodied ribs.

Determined, I rushed to the bathroom and dug into the small medicine cabinet on the wall. Hands full of alcohol bottles, cotton swabs and rolls of bandages, I hurried back to the bedroom where Jax was stripping off what was left of his shirt. *Fuck this man is gorgeous.* If the situation wasn't as dire as it was, I would have greedily explored his body with my tongue.

Shaking off the lewd thoughts, I placed the items on the bed and guided him to sit down, kneeling in front of him. He watched me with tired eyes, breathing heavily and grunting his disapproval as I began to clean the wound.

"You really don't have to do this."

"I do. I'm not just gonna let you bleed to death."

"Really, it's fine-"

"Stop saying that!"

Tears burned in my eyes threatening to spill. I pushed them back, inhaling air through my nose. Jax's reluctance to let me treat him did nothing to ease my worry.

He shuddered as I placed my hands on his thighs to make room for myself in between them, inching closer to him. Wrapping my arms around his neck, I pulled him down and placed a soft kiss on his lips before speaking quietly, not trusting my voice not to break.

"You are so stubborn, taking care of everyone. You look out for your crew, your people, your business, your family, everyone. And even me. You exhaust yourself thinking you have to fix everything by yourself."

"I have to-"

"Of course you do. That's who you are. There is nothing you can't do, and I admire that about you. That you are accomplished, successful, persistent and obsessive beyond comparison. You take care of everyone. But who takes care of you?"

Caressing his cheek, I rained kisses on his face, tenderly and slowly planting my lips on his skin, letting my feelings known; though I wasn't sure what those feelings were. *Love? Had I fallen in love with my husband? What else could it be?* Overwhelmed with the revelation, I kissed him deeply, making him groan as I pressed my body against him. *I was in love with Jax.*

"Let me take care of you." I whispered against his lips, feeling the tremors of his body from my words.

"Katy-."

"I'm your fucking wife! I'm doing this and you're gonna let me; or do I have to tie you to the bed so I can look at your wounds?"

"My wife is threatening me with a good time."

"Don't tempt me. I will fucking do it, and it's not gonna end the way you think it is."

"My cock buried deep in your pussy?"

My cheeks flushed red immediately and I pressed my thighs together to hide the wetness that began to slip into my panties. His nostrils flared and I noticed the shift in his gaze, looking down at me more hungry than before.

He said it as a matter of factly, like he knew I couldn't resist him, like I had already given my consent. Like that was his purpose all along, no matter the situation, I was gonna end up naked under him tonight. And damn it if that thought didn't turn me on. He nipped my ear, rewarding him with a soft moan I tried to hide by biting my lip, fruitless.

"Because that's exactly how this is going to end."

"Not till I'm done patching you up. So sit still and let me work."

"Okay."

Ignoring the clear effects of his arousal, I lathered the cotton swabs with alcohol and began the careful process of cleaning the blood around his wound. He didn't make a sound but I could feel him quiver under my touch as my fingers caressed his skin. The wound looked bad, whatever it was that hacked his skin, left it open with gnarly jagged edges.

"It needs stitches." I choked out, patting the dried blood around it.

"Then do it."

"I can't-"

"You can." He looked at me sternly. "There is a needle and a thread in that drawer over there."

"Jax, I don't know-"

"I've done it before. I'll guide you through it. I trust you." *Fuck.*

Climbing off the floor, I rushed to the desk in the corner and found the items he had mentioned. A bottle of fine whiskey sat on a tray on a shelf with a few glasses stacked next to it. I decided to grab that too. Returning, I shoved the bottle in his hand and knelt back down in front of him.

Taking a swig, he grunted his satisfaction at the gesture. There was no way of numbing the pain that was coming. Before I even had a chance to think about my trembling hands, he offered the bottle to me, too. A silent understanding passed between us. I placed the neck on my lips and took a big mouthful of the golden liquid. I hissed at the burning sensation falling down my throat and into my stomach.

"Easy there, it's vintage." His husky voice was like velvet, soothing the heating sensation spreading in my body. *How does one drink this stuff? Tastes like acid.*

"Noted." Coughing, I gave the bottle back to him and began to thread the needle with sturdier hands. I was in no way near qualified for doing this, and I told him as much, but Jax assured me that he wouldn't let the doctor or anyone else touch him. It had to be me. They always made it seem so easy in the movies, when the hero got hurt and somebody had to stitch them up.

Somehow I managed to sew his wound well enough for it to stop bleeding. It wasn't pretty by a long shot. I knew it would leave a nasty scar and the tattoos around it were ruined. He would have to get them fixed if he wanted the design to be whole again after the scar had healed.

In silence, I cleared the bed and floor from the stuff I had used to treat him and used the sink to wash the blood off my hands. It was even on my shirt that I tossed in the trash returning to the bedroom. Jax was still sitting on the edge of the bed.

"Come here." He coaxed with open arms. Like a moth to a flame, I floated across the room into his embrace and melted. His scent was incredible. Despite the disinfectant and blood, I could still smell the subtle hint of his musky sweat and aftershave.

I still had many questions but I knew it was not the time for a discussion, as his lips were peppering kisses and love bites down my neck. Climbing onto his lap, he wrapped his arms around me, molding our bodies together and grinding my pussy on his erection. Nothing but the fabric of our pants separated us.

My bra disappeared in a flash and his mouth dipped down to suck in my breasts. He paid attention special to the hardening peaks that he circled around with his tongue, sucking and nipping them with his teeth. With the flick of his tongue I became a panting mess, mewling on top of him like a cat in heat. I was sure my panties were completely soaked in my juices. His rock hard cock was pressing on my clit in the most delicious way and I knew I wouldn't last long if this continued.

"Oh God." A voice not my own moaned.

Jax released my breast with a pop and growled, sinking his fingers into my hair and tugging at the base, tilting my head.

"It's not a god that is making you feel good. You will scream my name and mine only. Do you understand?"

"Yes."

I almost got whiplash from how fast he flipped us over so my back hit the mattress. His hands ran down my stomach and in the next second he pulled my pants off and tossed them in the room somewhere. A sinister expression adorned his face, as though he was preparing to devour me.

"Spread your legs for me. Let me see that greedy pussy of yours."

My knees fell and I could feel the gush of my nectar leaking out of me, soaking my panties. The throbbing sensation had me drawing in a staggered breath in anticipation on what was to come. His pants came off just as fast as he had discarded mine and then he surged towards me, making me squeal.

His warm breath fanned over my pussy as he laid between my thighs. A shock raced over me as he licked me through the fabric. My hips moved on their own, grinding against his mouth seeking for more friction. I was so close to the orgasm I wanted to cry.

"Jax, please."

"Tell me what you want, wife." He rasped against my pussy, his voice vibrating on my sensitive skin.

"I need- Ah... more."

"Tell me. Use your words." His fingers teased the lacy edge of my panties, dragging it to the side and leaving my pussy bare for him to see. I shouldn't have felt shy, given the amount of times he had worshiped my pussy with his mouth and fingers, but still my cheeks heated up even more.

"Please... I need your fingers. I'm so close."

He hummed, pleased with my request. The lace ripped as he tore it off me and tossed the flimsy scraps over his shoulder. Then he brought his fingers up to my face, suggestively.

"Lick them."

They tasted like a mix of sweat and gunpowder with a hint of blood, a reminder of the grim events of today. I sucked and licked his fingers, hoping it would wash away some of the tainted memory and replace it with something better, something worth remembering.

Slathered in my saliva, he dragged the fingers down my body, stopping to tease my nipples and trailing down to my aching pussy. His thumb pressed on my clit, moving in a circle, at the same time as he sunk his digits inside me in one smooth motion. I was so drenched he slid into the last knuckle with ease. Pumping in and out of me, he curled his fingers, driving me insane with pleasure.

"Jax, I'm-"

"That's it, cum for me."

The tips of his fingers hit the spot that made me see stars as a precursor to the approaching orgasm. Titering on the edge of bliss had me screaming and moaning, thrusting my hips to meet his fingers that worked magic on my body.

"Now." He commanded.

And then I exploded. My orgasm hit me like a shock wave, surging through my body in droves. I trashed on the bed chasing the high, moaning and panting with abandon. Just when I thought I couldn't reach any higher, Jax curled his fingers and coaxed another, an even stronger eruption.

My juices gushed out like a fountain, but Jax was there to lap it all up. By kissing and stroking my pussy, he coached me through the climax till I sagged, heaving and spent on the sheets.

"You look absolutely gorgeous when you cum."

Jax crawled up my body, trailing his lips on my stomach, chest and neck. When he kissed me, I could taste myself, the salty sweetness seasoning his tongue. He wedged himself between my thighs, letting me feel how aroused he had gotten by rubbing his cock all over my pussy.

Reaching for his cock to stroke it, a little precum leaked out. He groaned, thrusting in my hand all the while whispering sweet nothings in my ear. The rumble of his voice sent shivers down my spine and straight to my core, igniting my desire for him. Coating his length with our mixed slicknes, I guided the head of his cock to my entrance, silently pleading.

With a small nudge of his hips, his cock sunk in me and I spread my thighs to make more room for him. His cock stretched me so well. Careful not to disturb the bandages around his torso, I pulled him against my chest as he buried himself to the hilt.

"So fucking tight."

His strong arms wrapped around me, pinning me down on the mattress and holding me in place, using me just the way he wanted. All I could do was gasp in response and cling to him when he started pistoning himself in and out of my pussy at a rapid pace. The sound of my moans drowned out the sound of our bodies sloshing together. Within minutes I could already feel another orgasm starting to crest.

I almost came when he sat up, changed the angle and started playing with my nipples, twisting them between his fingers. He palmed my breasts and toyed with the hard peaks, to his heart's content, till I was a weeping mess. Unsure if I could last much longer of his delicious torture, I hooked my legs behind his back, urging him to move faster.

With a wicked grin, he threw my legs over his shoulder, folding me in half and drove me over the edge. I felt my pussy clamp down and milk his cock as he roared his release with me. Even when both of us were truly spent and empty, he refused to stop moving inside me.

Letting my legs free, he leaned on his elbows, caging me between his thick biceps. It seemed like he couldn't stop touching and kissing me, lazily moving his hips and savoring the afterglow. The longer we stayed like that caressingly in each other's arms, I was certain, the swelling feeling in my chest was love.

I *loved* him. My husband. The devil himself.

Chapter 11

After the most passion filled night of my life, dawn seemed to creep up far too soon. Groggy and sore I tried to stretch but Jax's arm was tightly wrapped around my torso. He stirred and pulled me closer when I made a move to slip out of the bed.

"Where are you going, wife."

"Bathroom. I need to pee."

"Five more minutes."

"I can't."

With a disapproving growl he released me and I dashed to relieve myself. The reflection in the mirror resembled a cave woman more than myself. I didn't know my hair could hold so many knots and tangles. *My husband is an animal.*

Returning to the bedroom all washed and brushed awarded me with the beautiful sight of him laying on his back, slowly stroking himself. A mixture of a sigh and a moan left my mouth as I gazed upon him, licking my lips. A drop of dew formed between my legs and suddenly all sensations of sleepiness faded away.

"Good morning." I said, honey on my tone.

"Good morning. Now come back here so I can have you for breakfast."

I knew my cheeks were thick with blush but I couldn't stop the butterflies taking flight in my stomach. In seconds I found myself hoisted on top of him, my legs spread, my knees on both sides of his head as he began greedily feasting on my pussy.

This position put me in the perfect angle with his hips, aligning his cock with my mouth, which I took full advantage of. Dragging my tongue along his length and swirling it around the top rewarded me with his grunts and moans of pleasure. He in return, sucked and licked my pussy like he was starving, masterfully working me up to an orgasm.

Accepting the challenge to make him cum first, I wrapped my hand around his shaft, working it up and down with my mouth, while cupping his balls with the other. The rumble of his voice vibrated against my pussy lips, deliciously teasing me.

"Just like that. Don't stop."

I wasn't going to, in fact I planned on going above and beyond. Sucking at the tip of his cock hard, I focused my efforts both stroking him, tugging his balls and bringing my fingers to his hole. It puckered from my touch as I gently brought my saliva covered fingers to the opening and circled it.

"Fuck." Was all I was able to make out from him. He locked my thighs with his arms, pulling my pussy flush with his mouth like a seal. This man was determined to make me come in record time. My legs shivered and I released his cock from my mouth crying out, mad with pleasure. *Damn him.* This was going to be over in minutes.

Taking a deep breath, I sunk back on his cock, swallowing all the way down till his cock hit the back of my throat. The vibration of my moans made him go rigid below me. Just when I thought he would finish, he pushed on my hips so that I landed face first on the mattress between his legs.

With little effort, he shifted onto his knees and pressed himself against my ass. Looking over my shoulder, I came to realize just how right my description of him was. He looked wild, vigorous, full of raw power and dangerous, driven by pure lust and hunger for *me*. The thrilling sensation spread through my body like wildfire, igniting every nerve ending and heightening my senses.

Recklessly I wiggled my ass and hips in front of the beast that looked like he was ready to snap and pounce at me. A slap echoed on the walls before I even had time to react to it. A sharp scream ripped from my lungs. Again and again he painted my cheeks with his handprints, and I swear I came a little from just that.

Grabbing my hip with one hand and his cock with the other, he dragged the tip along my slit, coating himself with my arousal. Then, by pressing his cock against my ass, he teased the rim, mimicking what I did to him earlier, only I knew he wouldn't stop at teasing.

Despite the fury in his eyes, he remained perfectly still, silently asking for my consent, which I granted by pushing my hips towards him, forcing the tip to enter.

The sting had me hissing and biting the sheets, but he was gentle, letting me get used to the feeling of him in my ass. My pussy throbbed from the emptiness, jealous of how stuffed my ass was getting, inch by slowly inch.

"Brace yourself." Jax growled when my ass met his hips. He was now fully sheathed inside me and the stretch was almost too much for me to handle. Grabbing the end of the bed, I gave him a meek nod as he pulled himself completely out and slammed back inside.

My hips bucked from the force. With both of his hands on my hips, he rocked me back into him, setting the pace. The bed shook and groaned from the smashing of our bodies hitting together. His balls met my pussy with every thrust, slapping my clit, causing ripples of pleasure shooting up my spine.

My body convulsed and within minutes I found oblivion. Clinging to the edge of the bed I was sure I'd be thrown over it along with my earth shattering orgasm. Stars danced behind my lids and my cry of ecstasy joined the rhythmic pounding of our flesh.

Jax pulled me up so my back met his chest, wrapped his arm around my torso and placed the other on my neck. As I turned to look at him over my shoulder, he stole my lips into a furious kiss, his tongue playing with mine.

"One more." He murmured, biting my shoulder and dropping his hand to cup my pussy. I wasn't sure if I could come again after such a devastatingly strong orgasm. *Turns out I was wrong.* His hand worked wonders on my sensitive pussy, pumping in and out of me all the while never stopping the movements in my ass.

Despite feeling like a wet noodle, my orgasm kept building till I was a blubbering mess. Jax came harder than ever before, shooting his load in my ass while rubbing his fingers on my clit, drawing out my last orgasm to the verge of black out. When our drained bodies hit the bed, he remained inside me, savoring the connection.

I must have dozed off at some point and when I woke up again, the bed was empty. I assumed Jax had removed himself gently, used a washcloth to clean us both and covered me with the blankets before getting dressed and leaving for his duties.

Chapter 12

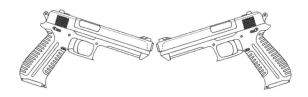

To my surprise, the house had turned into a refugee camp overnight. Every guest room was occupied and every soft surface served as a makeshift bed. The bathrooms seemed to be always occupied. Our food ran low in the first few days and someone had to venture out to get more supplies.

But it would have been insensitive to complain. These men risked their lives for me and my husband, ensuring the house remained safe and secure.

The men that had been wounded were recovering and their spirits remained high though hopeful. *I use the term lightly. I assume many of them are seeking revenge.*

There were of course some benefits to our situation as well. The house felt more lively than it had during my recovery and I wasn't feeling as lonely anymore. I could smell food being prepared practically every hour and the sounds of laughter made me almost believe we weren't in grave danger.

But above that, I got to see my husband more. I had missed him so much during his absence and we took every opportunity to make up lost time. If he wasn't down stairs elaborating plans with his men, we were entangled in each other's arms, often naked, that lead into hours of passionate lovemaking.

One day I noticed all of the men were hustling and bustling in the common area, cleaning and tidying up. I almost burst into whistling while they worked. Jax captured me under his arm as I approached him.

"What's going on?"

"Moving day."

"Oh?"

"Most of the men are recovered enough to move into different safehouses. It's uncommon to stay in one place for too long when we still don't know who leaked the security codes."

"Understandable." Giving him a light squeeze I tried to offer my support though I knew right now he was in his element, leading, planning and delegating. My presence wasn't needed but I wanted to be near him as much as possible, anyway. I bit my lip and turned the ring on my finger, unsure what my role was in all this. "What do you want me to do?"

"Pack."

"I'm leaving too?"

"Like I said, we can't stay in one place for too long. I just wanted to give you ample time to recover."

"I've been fine for days."

"I know-" Leaning over and lowering his voice so only I could hear, he continued. "-but I wanted you all to myself for a few days."

Hiding my face behind my hands, I mumbled something along the lines of 'I'll go up and start packing' and turned on my heels before anyone had time to notice the blush creeping up my face.

Not that there was much for me to pack since all my possessions were still at the penthouse. The few things I had accumulated in the past few days belonged to the house. I still spent a good ten or so minutes tidying up the rooms we had used, pocketed my toothbrush and knife, before returning downstairs with an armful of laundry.

Not long after, a caravan of blacked out SUVs were due to depart. Jax insisted I ride with him, which I didn't protest, of course, and buckled myself next to him with haste. To think a mere months ago it would have been the last thing on my wish list and now I couldn't get enough of him. *My husband.* I warped his trench coat tighter around me and inhaled his musky scent.

I had no memory of the road that led to the house. For the next hour my eyes wandered over the unfamiliar landscape in an attempt to recognize any of the landmarks. Another hour passed before I was able to identify some of the road names.

I was about to ask where we were headed, but when I glanced over at Jax, I saw his serious expression, focused, intent on the road ahead, so I decided against it. Instead, I stayed silent, gazing out into the distance, trusting that he knew the way.

My questions were quickly answered when he made a turn off the road and came to a stop at a roadside grill. Leaving the engine running he stepped out of the car and motioned me to follow him. He was already at the booth when I managed to climb out of the car and scanned our surroundings. The place looked deserted, just a forgotten pitstop between the trees and the road.

A cold breeze blew through the crowns, making them sway and hum quietly. There was something eerie about this place making a shiver run down my spine. The grill looked like it had been abandoned a long time ago based on the rust on the window panes. I stepped over the weeds growing from the cracks in the dirt covered concrete.

When Jax returned, he was tapping away on his phone. Before I had time to ask my question, he had already closed the distance between us and placed a fleeting kiss on my cheek.

"There is a tower a few miles from here, the only place there is cell service in this whole county."

"So you left the house to come here?"

"Yes. I had other things I needed to take care of but this was the closest place to keep in contact with the people I knew I could trust." His phone buzzed again and his brows creased looking at it.

"Oh, I understand. Like a safe hot spot."

He hummed in response, stepping away from me and leaning on the hood of the car, tapping his reply to the incoming messages. Though there was no snow on the ground, the air was still nippy. I dug my hands into the jacket pocket and pulled out a lighter and a pack of cigarettes, placing one on his lips and lighting it up. His eyes gleamed in the soft orange glow of the embers. It reminded me of the night we first met.

I let out a sigh. *Love. This is definitely love.* What I thought had been the worst night of my life turned out to be one of the best. I couldn't believe I ever thought kissing this man was a mistake. He was *mine*.

Distracted with my thoughts, I didn't notice the caravan of blacked out cars turning off the road until they stopped right next to us. Questioning, I turned to Jax, but he remained unphased, as if he had expected them. A handful of armed men funneled out of the vehicles and stood guard surrounding us. I had to do a double take to realize who stepped out of the last car.

"Papa?" I couldn't believe my eyes. He stood there with open arms, smiling, like this was a normal event. Like last time he saw me, hadn't been terrifying for me. Like he hadn't beaten me within the inch of my life the night of the wedding. Like he could just walz out here and expect me to not resent him for it.

"Valentina. Come here, malyshka."

My feet didn't move. I couldn't. I wouldn't. I was frozen in place, trying to decipher the situation. *How is he here? And why?* Feeling my pulse spike, I began to fidget with my ring once more, turning it in my finger in an attempt to ground myself. I couldn't understand what was going on.

His smile fell slightly and I could see the shift in his posture. Snapping out of my trance I forced my feet to move. With great effort I managed a delighted expression to form on my face. I knew better than to anger my father, especially when we were outnumbered. His arms closed around me, pulling me in and patting my back, strangely welcoming. When we parted, I laced my voice with as much honey as possible but I felt my smile failing.

"It's good to see you, Papa."

"Malyshka, I've missed your subtle venom."

"No, I mean it. I just wasn't expecting to see you so soon." *If ever. I'd be perfectly happy if I never see another member of the bratva ever again. But alas, here he is.*

"The feeling is mutual, unfortunately the situation has changed. Are you ready?"

"Uh.. ready for what?"

"To leave of course. I've come to collect you."

"To collect- what? No, wait."

"It's cold, malyshka. We can't stay here all day. Come on now. Get in the car." My father held my arm firmly and began to lead me to the back.

The men surrounding us made their move as well and started funneling back into their vehicles. Frantically, I looked towards my husband seeking his aid, but he remained still, lazily smoking his cigarette. His expression was unreadable and it scared me. *How is he okay with this?*

"Wait wait wait, just hold on for one second. Jax? Explain." Nothing. He said nothing, made no move to comfort me nor to protect me. He remained still, like he didn't care if I was in his life. *It can't be.*

"Don't worry about him, it's all sorted with the O'Haras." My father retorted, ignoring my protest as I struggled in his hold. His fingers felt bruising, digging into my flesh, giving me flashbacks to that fateful night. "They won't be expecting a payment for terminating the contract early."

"Jax?" It felt like everything else faded away and my vision narrowed only on Jax. Calling out for him again, I managed to snap my arm away from my fathers grasp and take one staggering step back. "No, let go. I have to hear it from him. Is it true?"

"Yes." When he finally spoke, his voice was low and harsh, just like before, just like the day we met. Sharp like ice. My heart shattered. *No.* "You will go with your father and be with your family."

"I don't understand. Why? Please, explain." The silent plea for reason did not reach him. He seemed colder, distant, void of emotions, like this didn't matter. Like I didn't matter to him.

"The threat on your life hasn't been eliminated. This

is a precaution. I made a deal with your father to take you back, under the condition that you'd be relocated to another safehouse out of the country."

"Are you serious?" Swallowing the tears that threatened to spill, I hoped it would not be true. I hoped what my father said was a lie and I hoped Jax would stop him from taking me. But his expression told me otherwise. There was no regret there. They were simply empty.

"Yes, it has been decided."

Those words rung in my head, shaking me to my core. I couldn't believe what I was hearing. This was not the man that had me in his bed only a few hours ago, this was not the man that had kissed me like he loved me. This was not the man I had given my heart to. *How could he throw me away?*

"Bullshit! You can't decide that. What about what I want? Did you ever stop to consider what I want?"

"What you want is irrelevant. This is for the best. It's for your safety."

And just like that, I was back in that room, on Christmas eve, and someone else, *a man*, was making my life choices for me. I couldn't accept that, not again.

"I'll be safe with you. I'm your *wife-*" I said quietly, desperately trying to reap air into my lungs.

"You were a *convenience*. A means to an end, nothing more. It's stupid to think otherwise."

"Please don't do this." My voice cracked, turning into a meek whisper that made its way past my lips. My entire body was shaking, that had nothing to do with the cold. I was surprised I was still able to stand. The forest was spinning and the air felt like ice.

Jax stomped his cigarette and put the final nail to my

coffin. "I'm done talking about this. You will go. End of. My decision is final."

I closed my eyes, not wanting to see him walk away and let the tears fall silently. There was no dignity in crying in front of people. I knew this. I knew I wouldn't receive any sympathy for showing weakness but I was at the end of my rope. My body numb, I climbed into the car and slammed the door on my heart.

Chapter 13

*D*enial. I couldn't believe what had happened. It wasn't real. It couldn't be real. Our marriage was over, I knew this, but I still refused to believe it to be true. Everything happened so fast. It didn't feel real.

Dazed and exhausted, I was like a zombie. If someone were to ask me how I got to the safe house, I couldn't tell. Half the time I was asleep, trying to escape the pain that came when I was awake. All I could do was cry and wallow in my sorrow.

Ridiculous as it may seem, there was still a glimmer of hope in my heart that it was all just an elaborate ruse, a joke, some twisted prank. But when I woke up in a strange bed, alone, I knew there was no hope to redeem our relationship.

Anger. There are no words strong enough to describe how I was feeling. I felt broken, destroyed, wounded, ripped open and raw. I was hurting in the worst possible way and I took it out on everyone around me.

Due to the tropical spring rain, I spent most of the days

inside the villa that served as our safe house. I still had no clue where we were, but I had a sneaking suspicion we were somewhere close to where we used to go on a holiday when I was younger. When mom was still alive. Those holidays were rare and far between, but I had a vague memory of the beach and the ocean.

Being stuck inside had its benefits as the villa had a huge indoor gym which I took full advantage of. While using a punching bag to get rid of some of the frustration, I asked myself the burning questions 'why?'

Why would he do this? Why would he lie to my face? Why did he make me believe he actually cared two shits about me? Why would he string me along if he meant to get rid of me anyway? Why was I still in love with him? Why can't I ever just be happy?

I punched harder. *Why. Won't. He. Get. Out. Of. My. Head?* Punching between every word, harder and harder, beating up the bag as it swung in the air, taking my anger as if it would make me feel any better. It didn't. Nothing would make it better.

Bargain. For a fleeting moment I thought I was at fault, that I had done something wrong. I vowed that I would be better, do better from now on. Maybe then there would still be a future for us. I would be the perfect wife, the perfect doll the men always wanted.

Quiet, fit, polished, well mannered, mindfull, demure, submissive, prim and proper.

I shuddered at the thought. That would not be my fate. That wasn't me, and maybe that was the problem. I wasn't perfect. Maybe if I had been, he would have loved me. He wouldn't have thrown me a way. Maybe if I was her, the perfect daughter, the perfect bride, I'd deserve his love. Maybe, just maybe if I could be *her*. But I'll never be her.

Depression. As the days turned into weeks and weeks into months, I seemed to have lost all of my energy. The weather, unlike my mind, stayed sunny, and instead of enjoying the tropical weather, I made a nest for myself in one of the guest rooms. All I wanted to do was to hide away in the cocoon and disappear. The world seemed to be drained of all colors, all light, all laughter, all happiness and life just gone. I felt nothing but the void inside me.

I even lost my appetite. My father had to hire a nutritionist that was in charge of my daily intake of all the nutrients. I didn't care if I wilted away. It was all the same to me. Nothing mattered.

He tried everything. He even thought bringing my cousin Erica to the villa would cheer me up. It didn't. She was in love and *happily married* to her husband, Francisco Lorenzo. Her marital bliss practically oozed out of her. I would have hated her for it if I had any energy to hate.

They even hosted a recreation of their wedding at the villa. She looked just like me if only slightly shorter, with similar hair, ears and nose all of our family members seemed to inherit.

Shamelessly she flaunted her ring in front of everyone. I hated every second of it. Their cheerful attitude was a constant reminder of what I had lost. I couldn't even muster a fake smile in most of the pictures taken that day.

Acceptance. He was gone. The grief would take its time, but I had to move on, however long it would take, I'd be whole again. *Maybe.*

The day my cousin showed her sonogram I realized I had to snap out of my misery. I had to make peace with the loss and focus on the future. Our family was going to

get a new member and I needed to be supportive. I was
going to be an aunt.

Chapter 14

The baby bump on Erica's abdomen caught my attention as I relaxed on the patio in the warm weather. She was showing more every day and practically glowing, ready to pop. Her husband adored her and catered to her every whim and craving. He had just brought us both some refreshing drinks and sat down to rub her feet. She moaned and let her head fall back, enjoying the princess treatment she was given.

I decided it was time for me to retreat indoors. There was only so much I could take. I was jealous. Looking at them only made me think of what I could have had if things wouldn't have turned out the way they did. It had been months since I allowed myself to think of *him*, and it still stung.

On my way to the kitchen, I heard my father beckon me from his office, wiping the sweat off his forehead with a handkerchief. His Hawaiian shirt was half open, revealing the gold chains that adorned his stubby neck and hairy chest.

"Malyshka, glad I caught you, Come, sit with us." I could

tell he was missing our winter home in Moscow. Stepping into the study, I noticed Logan already lounging in one of the wicker chairs. He was casually smoking a cigar and taking a sip of his iced scotch.

"Privyet. What is it?"

"Sadites', Valentina."

Taking the seat across from my father, my eyes darted between the two of them. Something in the back of my mind was prickling and it had nothing to do with the air condition unit blaring in the corner.

"It's been almost a year we've been on this island." He began, fanning himself with a magazine. I simply nodded, waiting for him to continue. "I know it hasn't been easy to be away from our homes, but that is about to change."

"Change? You mean we are going back?"

"Yes." Pausing for dramatic effect, he lifted his glass to his lips and emptied his drink. "Logan here has assured me that he and his crew have eliminated the threat."

I knew it. There had to be a reason he was in this conversation. I glanced over to him only to find him already staring back at me. His hungry eyes raked over my body as he licked his lips, making my skin crawl. Suppressing a shiver I shifted my attention back to my father, who was already filling another glass.

"That is good news then."

"It's wonderful news. I've just about had enough of all this fucking sunshine." He said. Still unsure why I had been summoned, I turned the ring on my finger. It felt loose on my skinny finger. "Which brings me back to you, malyshka."

"What of me?"

"I've decided you shall be wed, again."

"What?" -*the fuck. Not again.*

"To Logan. He was gracious enough to only ask you as payment for his services."

"I'm not some toy you can bargain off."

He pinched the bridge of his nose. "Not this again. How many times do you plan on contesting me before you learn your lesson? Need I remind you what happened last time you disobeyed me?"

"No, but-"

"I'm not having this argument with you again! You and Logan will get married." His fist met the table with a bang, making a dent in the wood. I almost leaped out of my seat when his bloodshot eyes met mine with a familiar fury. "Show him some gratitude. He has risked his life for your safety. Your submission is a small price for that."

My stomach hollowed and my fingers dug into the hand rest for support. *How many times would I have to endure being someone's puppet?* I was trapped in a never ending circle of being passed around like some token, a trophy. My breathing was so loud I barely registered what Logan was saying to me.

"Valentina, I promise you, I'll be good to you. I've spent this year building our future. You'll have nothing to worry about, ever. I'll keep you safe."

His honed words slithered over my skin like venom, turning my blood into ice. Something about the way he reached over and grabbed my hand had my heart racing in the wrong way. He promised me safety and security. I'd be taken care of, be covered in riches and bathe in his wealth. He would keep me sated, forever.

A gilded cage is still a cage.

The thought was suffocating.

When I thought I'd have all those things, it wasn't Logan's face I imagined, it was Jax. *He* was the one that haunted my dreams. He was the one still holding my heart. With him, I didn't feel trapped. This was not right. I simply could not go through with another marriage while I still had a glimmer of hope. I had to see him one last time.

"May I ask for one thing?"

"Of course. Anything for my future wife." *Cringe.*

"I wish to see Jackal O'Hara."

"Why?" His eyes narrowed. The jealousy practically oozed out of him like a dark shadow, as his grip tightened on my hand.

"I want to be sure our marriage is truly over."

"What do you mean 'truly over'? You think he would want you back after all this time when there is nothing to gain from it? That's ridiculous."

"Maybe, but I demand to see him."

"Is this some trick? It's over, Valentina. Just accept it." My father added.

"Not until I see him." Standing up and rounding the desk, I approached my father, pleading for my life. I was not above begging. I got down on my knees in front of him, something I hadn't done before. "Do this one thing, this one and only thing I ask of you, please, Papochka."

"I do this and you will marry Logan, no arguments, no fighting, no back talk. Not a single word or action out of line. You will behave and be nice to your husband and do as you're told."

"Yes. I promise. I'll do anything he wants, just grant me this one wish."

"Anything?"

"Yes, anything."

He leaned back in his chair, crossed his fingers above his chest and looked down at me, puzzled. The minutes ticked by and I fought the urge to move as I felt the pins and needles creeping up my legs. Just when I thought he would refuse, he let out a big sigh.

"Very well. When we get back, I will arrange a meeting with Mr. O'Hara. Till then, you better be on your best behavior or else-"

"Yes, Papa. Spasibo." I jumped to my feet and kissed him on both cheeks.

The deal was sealed.

Chapter 15

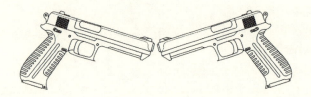

Black and white. The streets glistened where the snow had melted, reflecting the lights of the billboards on the black pavement. Frost laid on top of every surface the cold had touched, crystalizing and painting the city white. A thick blanket of snow had fallen overnight. Dead branches swayed and shivered, twisting in the wind, whispering to the silent city.

It was warm in the car, but I still felt cold sweat run down my spine. I pressed my hands between my thighs to stop myself from fidgeting. The headlights burned in my retina, shining towards the middle of the parking lot where my father was already standing outside with his entourage, dressed in black, fully armed and in position to greet our guest.

Logan squeezed my knee, slightly harder than was necessary. I bristle at his touch. Ever since that conversation, he had gotten more aggressive with his approach. He was clingy and more forceful than before. He was acting as if we were already married and I had to use every ounce of my charm and skills to keep him at arm's length but content, lest I anger him. It was getting harder every day to turn him down. Every kiss made the bile rise in my throat.

"Remember, Valentina, not a word."

"I promised I would be good."

His hand moved up my thigh, his thumb following the seam of my pants. I shuffled in my seat in an attempt to shake him off gently, but his hand carried on, till it rested on my hip, bruisingly. In my head I prayed he wouldn't move any further.

"Well, just to make sure you keep your word, I placed snipers in the surrounding buildings." His face turned into a sinister smirk and indicated towards the rooftops. I stared at him in horror, not wanting to believe what he said to me.

"What?" I squeaked, feeling my heart in my throat.

"You keep your mouth shut and the pretty boy gets to keep his head. Do you understand? One word out of your mouth and-" He imitated the sound of an explosion with his mouth while mimicking the effects with his hand next to his skull.

"Are you serious?"

"Deadly serious. Don't test me, Valentina." He replied, snaking his hands up my torso, cupping my breast. Mentally I willed my body not to recoil. I wanted to punch him so hard I had to hold on to the leather seat not to go through with it. He got closer, his breath fanning over the skin on my neck.

"You don't need to do this."

"I beg the differ. You have a tendency to fuck things up." He nipped my lip, causing me to yelp.

"What are you talking about?"

I pushed him back and noticed him licking his lips,

tasting my blood. No longer able to hide my fury, I scowled at him, but before I had a chance to do anything else, he reached for the door to unlock it.

"They're here. Get out."

Stumbling out of the car, I wrapped my coat tighter around myself, feeling the cold winter breeze whip my hair immediately. Everywhere I looked was concealed in the darkness. The endless cover of the clouds shrouding what would have been a beautiful star lit sky. The lights pouring out the windows created a patchwork of illuminated squares against the harsh shadows of the buildings. No sign of snipers, though, but I knew that was by design.

Logan moved beside me and I felt him press the parallel of a gun at my back. "Remember, not a sound."

The tone in his voice was enough of a threat without the added pressure on my back, because what he had revealed in the cabin had already sealed my lips. Despite what had happened, despite everything we went through, I wouldn't risk Jax's life. He was the one thing I couldn't sacrifice.

The headlights of the other caravan shined brightly, joining the already existing halo. My pulse was hammering a mile a minute in my throat almost deafeningly loud. Squinting, I tried to recognize any of the faces of the men stepping out of the vehicles. Only when I was almost certain this was a set up, I saw *him*.

He was as handsome as I remembered. Tall, dark and mysterious, the deep contours carving his face. The ember of his cigarette brought a red glow to his eyes. I bit my lip as our eyes locked. He was gorgeous and I cursed my treacherous heart for thumping faster because of it. Even now, even after all this time, I was still madly in love with him. And for a second, I thought I saw something in his expression too.

But just as fast, the moment was gone. He looked away and focused on my father, stepping forth, a respectable distance from everyone. The spotlight was on the two of them. Out of a habit, I played with the ring on my finger. The ring I hadn't had the heart to get rid of. Not yet.

"Mr. Gregorovich." Hearing his voice for the first time in almost a year was a shock to my system. Involuntary moan threatened to escape me. His voice was a low rumble, like velvet for my senses, bringing back all the memories of how it affected me. *Damn.*

"Mr. O'Hara. Priviet. Glad you could join us."

"So, you've summoned me. Let's skip the pleasantries."

"Quite right. It's rather cold out and I'm sure we would rather be at home than freezing our asses off."

"Indeed."

"Straight to the point then." Vapors formed in the air as they spoke. "You and I both know your relationship with my Valentina ended abruptly due to some unfortunate circumstances." *To put it mildly.*

"I'm aware. I thought the matter settled. We are not currently under a new contract nor do we have any joint business that need such insurance."

Snowflakes got caught in my lashes but I didn't dare to blink as I noticed a red dot that had appeared on Jax's jacket. *Shit.* As the conversation carried on, more dots joined the first.

"My question is, do you wish to resume this marriage?"

"This is why you summoned me?"

"It had to be settled. For our families to keep on working together in good faith in the future, I had to be sure of your stance on the matter. It's only good business."

"I believe my answer remains unchanged so it's not up to me to decide. If *Valentina* wishes to return, she should speak for herself." My name felt like daggers. He had never used my first name before. *What did he mean by that? Is he trying to send me a message or am I just overthinking it?*

"Well, do you, malyshka? Do you wish to return to your husband?" Both of them turned to face me. My father issued a silent warning but Jax remained unreadable, yet again. He was being cryptic when I needed him to be clear. For once I wished there would be no secrets between us. No more lies, no more guessing what the other one was thinking. I didn't know what was real anymore.

Do I wish to go back to the man I loved?

Yes. The voice in my head screamed.

"*Shake your head.*" Logan hissed in my ear so no one else could hear and poked the barrel of the gun against my spine. The red dots on Jax's jacket were aimed at his heart. Slowly, I complied, shaking my head from side to side. If Jax was disappointed, he didn't show it as he turned away.

"This was a waste of time."

"Glad we agree. Consider this matter settled once and for all. I do hope when we meet again it will be more beneficial to the both of us. Dasvidaniya."

Jax didn't meet my gaze again. He simply nodded to my father, motioned his men to retreat and climbed into his car. Logan might as well have shot me. I felt like a bullet had just pierced my heart. It was finally over.

This time, I didn't cry. I had no more tears to give. As their tail lights disappeared into the frozen flurry, I accepted my fate. I feared I would no longer be able to deny Logan. He would have me with or without my consent. A bullet may have been more merciful.

Chapter 16

"**D**o you Valentina Katerina Gregorovich take Logan Hunter as your lawfully wedded husband?"

"I do." My voice cracked. I didn't even bother to hide it. Fear had slithered its way to my chest and made a nest there.

The ceremony was even quicker than last time. The officiant rushed through our vows like he was being threatened by the goons acting as our witnesses, which he probably was. I had no doubt Logan had anticipated the course of the events and made the officiant wait in the room for our arrival.

"Then by the power-"

"Didn't I say we were in a hurry."

"But, sir-"

"Sign it." Logan tapped on the marriage certificate laying on the desk in front of us with his gun. "Don't make me repeat myself."

The smell of urine filled the room as the officiant took the pen in his shaky hand and inked the bottom of the paper, making the marriage official and legal. When he was done, Logan snapped the pen from his hand and forced it into mine. I hesitated for a second. Logan growled, fisting my hair and bending me over the desk so my cheek was flush with the paper.

"Logan, you're hurting me." I cried.

"Sign. It."

Hastily, I scribbled my name on the line before he followed suit. When it was done, he pulled me against him and planted a bruising kiss against my lips, sticking his tongue so far in my throat it made me gag. My feeble struggles against his grasp only spurred him on more.

"You're mine." He roared, biting my lip before turning to the others.

"Your services are no longer needed. Get out!" His voice reverberated on the walls, leaving no room for argument. The officiant got practically thrown out by the goons. As the door slammed shut after them, I stood alone in the room with Logan, with no social armor to protect me from him.

"Take off your clothes." He growled, loosening his tie and unbuttoning his shirt.

"What? No."

"You think I'm joking? Take off your fucking clothes, Valentina, or I will do it for you."

When I refused, he closed the distance between us in one long stride. In the next second he was on me, wrestling my arms I had raised to block him. He grabbed a hold of my wrist and twisted, causing me to yelp out. At that moment I really wished I had something to stab him with. My lips, neck and jaw felt sore as his attempts to kiss me fell short and he ended up biting me instead.

"Stop it." I tried knowing full well he wouldn't.

"I've waited long enough. For years you've been nothing but a cock tease. It's time to pay up."

"Don't touch me."

"I can do whatever the fuck I want. You belong to me and I'm going to fuck every hole in your body till you get it in your thick fucking scull that I own you. You're *mine*."

The back of my knees met the edge of the bed, causing me to fall back on the mattress. The air left my lungs as he threw his entire body weight on top of me. Scrambling to get away from him, I kneed him in the groin, which seemed to have no effect on him. It only spurred him on. I punched, kicked and screamed with all my might trying to shake him.

"Please stop! Get off me!"

Using my hips for leverage, I managed to stagger him long enough to make his nose bleed, before he had me pinned under him again. Unaffected by my protest he continued the assault and used his much larger size to his advantage. He dominated the fight and in a matter of minutes, I was trapped. Despite my best efforts to get free, he secured my arms to the headboard with the tie.

"Stop fighting. This will hurt a lot less if you just play along."

I could feel his fingers digging into my clothes, pulling and ripping them at the seams. Squirming, wiggling and twisting my body I made feeble attempts to shake him. My fight was fizzling out along with my voice, that had become nothing but a pathetic sob.

"Don't-"

"Bitch! I'm going to put a bullet to your fucking head if you don't stop fighting."

The cold metal met my temple, pushing me deeper into the mattress as I recoiled. I swallowed the fractions of my pride and seized the struggle. I was not able to stop the tears from falling, though.

"Now be a good little slut, and let me fuck you like the dirty little whore you are. I hope that bastard didn't ruin you for me."

The cool air hit all over my body as he tore off what little was left of my clothes. He dragged his tongue along my exposed skin, making it prickle with goosebumps. I could tell he was pleased with how my body was reacting, as I felt his hard on pressing against my thigh. He massaged my breast briefly before pinching my nipple, painfully twisting and pulling it beyond its limit. I hissed in pain and before I could stop myself, I spat on his face.

"Stupid, bitch."

Instead of a bullet, he hit me with the blunt handle of the gun in the face. It hurt like a motherfucker and I knew he had broken something. Then he hit me again. And again. The taste of copper filled my mouth. I must have blacked out for a moment, because when I came to, I felt agonizing pain and I was covered in blood. Dazed from the blows and tears clouding my vision, I fell limp on the covers, finally admitting I was too weak to fight him off anymore.

His weight left my body only for a moment. When he returned, he was naked and clammy from sweat. I sobbed silently. Tremors rumbled through my body like a wave. He climbed on top of me, forcing my knees to part. My stomach lurched and I closed my eyes, wishing for death.

Don't do this. Please. Anything but this.

Death was banging at the door.

No, please please please.

Make it stop. Please.

The booming sound rattled in my head, deafening.

Please make it stop.

Not like this. Stop it.

The noise only got lounder.

Please.

And louder.

No.

Please.

Boom!

Glass shattered, cold air rushed in and the weight on my body disappeared. On instinct I shriveled into a ball trying to shield myself from the freezing air. Somehow I managed to wiggle out of my restraints. Dark figures danced in my vision, moving like a rabid beast. Logan's gun lay discarded on the mattress and I reached for it, taking aim at the new threat.

One of the dark figures split from the rest. I blinked, reeling in some clarity to my vision. It was too damn cold to focus on anything else but the jittering of my teeth. The gun swayed in my hand, my finger frozen on the trigger. Through the commotion, a deep voice called out to me.

"Katy."

"D-don't c-come any c-closer. I'll s-shoot."

"Then shoot me, make me bleed, it's what I deserve. Just let me hold you."

The soft tone penetrated my defenses, stirring me awake, granting me the soft touch of familiarity. Safety. I didn't think I'd get to see his face ever again. He was here. He came for me. He saved me.

"I... Oh God. Jax." A horace cry rattled in my throat as I fell into his arms and sobbed against his shirt. The warmth of his body engulfed me and I clung to him like he was my lifeline, like I was afraid he would disappear. I felt his arms wrapping me in his tight embrace, cradling me to his chest.

"Hush. I've got you. I'm here. I'm sorry I was late. You're safe. He can't hurt you anymore." His words lulled my nerves. I felt the sincerity, the raw emotions that he poured into his vows. "It's over. I won't let anything happen to you. I promise. I will never leave you again. Ever. They will have to take you from my cold dead hands before I let that happen."

I believed him. Carried in the comfort of his arms, I pressed my ear against his chest, feeling the soothing rhythm of his heart. The beat matched my own. I was not afraid anymore.

Chapter 17

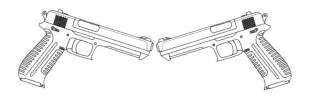

Hours earlier

"Boss?"

I snapped out of my thoughts. The weather was less than ideal for what we were about to do. As soon as I had received the message from Mr. Gregorovich, I started planning.

It was strange why the meeting was set out doors, when I was sure we all would have preferred to remain indoors. Nobody in their right minds would have requested an audience in the dead of winter, unless they had ulterior motives.

"Is everything ready?"

"Yes. Everyone is geared up and waiting for your command, sir."

A neat selection of finely polished handguns lay on the wooden desk. I had yet to select the iron I would use as I had gotten distracted by the thoughts of *her*, again.

"Good. This can't go wrong. You understand what's at line here? If all else fails, I'm counting on you to be our last resort."

"Of course. I won't fail you."

"*She* is your top priority."

"You have my word, boss. She saved me once. I owe my life to her."

"Then it's time to go. Good luck, Petras."

Though I trusted my men I had hand selected for this mission, none of them came even close to Petras. He out of all of them had the most to prove. He had survived a near death experience, and through a long recovery and rehabilitation, he was back in action, ready to pay his debt. His eagerness and skills were the exact reason why I chose him to lead the sniper team.

Of course, at first I couldn't be sure there would be a need for snipers, but with a little research of the surrounding area of the meeting place, I discovered a major disadvantage to whomever stood in it. The layout was open, bare, and offered little to no cover in case of a fight. The surrounding buildings were tall, covering every side except the entrance road, making it perfect conditions for an ambush.

Only a fool would enter without preparation and back up. Knowing full well how the minds of my enemies worked, had me believe they would do exactly what I expected them to do. I would have my men already positioned in the buildings before theirs even arrived.

Then it would be my turn to play the part. Pulling the coat over myself and heading down stairs, my thoughts went to *her*. It had been months since I last saw Katy, but that didn't mean I hadn't kept my eye on her. My informants had given me regular updates on her whereabouts, ensuring me she was well taken care of, otherwise I would have intervened sooner.

Her family had relocated to the south to a villa not far

from where she vacationed as a child. A story she had shared with me during one of our date nights. It was fairly easy to place my informants as employees at their safehouse to keep tabs on them.

At first Katy had been unwell and distraught of our separation, rightfully so, and it pained me to have caused her that. *Soon, I'd repay her for all the suffering she went through because of me.* For weeks the reports I got were nothing but snippets of how her mental state had not changed. It almost made me abort the mission and abandon our goal.

But when I received the wedding pictures, I gained a renewed sense of purpose. The wedding seemed small enough but sent a clear message, that she was moving on with her life. I couldn't accept that.

Originally my plan was to have her move to safety and eliminate the threat, but despite my best efforts, I still had no idea who was behind the hitmen. I worked tirelessly, combed the city, tore through the underground, fought, killed and bribed, and still ended up with nothing. I couldn't bring Katy back knowing she would still be in danger. I had to bide my time and double my efforts.

A month later my informants delivered early sonogram pictures. They made me realize things were moving a lot faster than I had anticipated. I was on borrowed time. My suspicion was that the Gregoroviches would not be moving during the pregnancy, which gave me a deadline.

I imagined her, how beautiful she was, the way she laughed and the softness of her lips. She occupied my every waking thought, and at night when I took my cock in my hand, she was there in my dreams as well.

Time passed, the seasons changed and I had finally made a breaking discovery. As expected, my informants sent me new images from the villa. The baby bump had grown large over the summer. According to my calculations, at some point in November, the baby would have reached its due date.

I grew anxious by the day knowing I'd see her soon. It became harder to hide my obsession with her. Because that's what I was, obsessed, completely consumed by her. Some days I felt like I couldn't breathe because she wasn't with me. Every day was like torture. But it was about to end.

About a month ago, my informants returned from their post giving their finished report as their targets had returned from hiding. Imagine my surprise when one of them gave me the final piece of the puzzle I had been looking for. The movements and dealings of one Mr. Logan Hunter.

Finally coming to the conclusion of who had been behind all the misdeeds. Digging deeper into his background, not only was he meddling with my business but several other mob families' as well. It wasn't hard to convince them to cooperate in taking down this hydra of a snake. Double crossing, insider trading, sabotage, corruption and theft were only a few of his crimes. Clearly he had no honor, no sense of loyalty to anyone.

Logan Hunter was a filthy rat and he had his claws on my Katy. *My wife.*

I'm going to fucking kill that bastard.

I picked the engraved glock with a silver finish and filled it with bullets, before securing it in its holster, right next to my heart. An extra set of magazines were tucked in my belt in case I needed them. And I was gonna need them. Lighting up my cigarette, I watched the live security footage of the parking lot where a handful of cars were waiting for us. It was show time.

Chapter 18

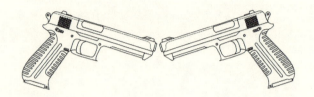

My wife safely in my arms, I wasted no time taking her to the new house. After I had washed her, I placed her in my bed and watched over her while the doctor checked her injuries. My fingers itched to bring back the bastard that did that to her only to kill him again.

Had I been a minute too late, he would have violated her in the most unforgivable way. According to the doctor, *physically* he hadn't succeeded. All her wounds indicated she fought hard to prevent it. *Mentally*, however, he couldn't be sure. That remained to be seen. I would be with her while she recovered. I was prepared to do anything and everything for her. I'd give my life for her. That was my silent vow.

Getting up from my chair I had remained the entire night, I walked to the window and pushed aside the curtain. It was late in the afternoon, the sky was clear and I could see the garden covered in white. The pale light of the sun streamed through the crack, illuminating the room.

When she finally came too it was already way past noon the next day. She stirred in her sleep and I moved to the edge of the bed, brushing the hair off her face, careful not to disturb the bandages. Her brows furrowed and a quiet whimper left her lips. I had no doubt she was reliving the nightmare.

Kissing her forehead, I made the attempt to arouse her awake gently. With a groan, her sleep filled eyes fluttered open. Her focus wandered till she met my gaze and she let out a sigh. The sweetest smile creeped to her face, lighting up my world again. I had been in the dark for far too long.

"Jax?"

"I'm here."

"Was it all a bad dream?"

"I'm afraid not."

"Did he-?"

Her voice trembled and almost cracked. Turning her head, she tried to hide the tears forming in the corner of her eyes. Placing a finger under her chin, I made her look at me before swiping them away with my thumb. She didn't need to hide them from me. I had seen all of her and I loved everything about her. I loved *her*.

"No. He didn't. We got to you just in time."

"And is he?"

"Dead? Yes." I said, my voice low, almost unable to contain the satisfaction he had died by my hand. Petras' bullet had wounded him, paralyzing him in an instant, but I was the one that put the bullet in his head, ending his miserable life by spreading his brains all over the floor.

Taking her hands in mine, I kissed her bony knuckles. She had lost a lot of weight in the time we spent apart. I made a mental note to take her to the best restaurants in the city so she could regain her strength.

"Pitty. I wanted to do it myself."

A choked out laugh had my face tugging in a smile. My wife was a viper. She was ready for vengeance even in the state that she was in. I couldn't deny that the thought of her covered in our enemies blood had my cock hardening in an instant.

"You'll have your revenge. I promise you. Once you've recovered, I have something you can take your anger on."

"Sounds good."

As she sighed again, she made room in the bed for me to join her. Crawling next to her, my arm circled her stomach and pulled her against me. She smelled like jasmine and vanilla. *God, I had missed her.*

"How are you feeling?" I whispered against her hair. She squirmed, rubbing her face against my chest and digging her hands under my shirt.

"Better with you here."

"Then I shall stay for as long as you need."

"How about forever?"

"I promised you, I'd never leave you again."

"Back at the parking lot. The way you acted, I thought you didn't want me." *Insane thought.*

"Of course I did. And I do. I would have given anything to take you back sooner. If it were up to me I would have thrown you over my shoulder then and there."

"Why didn't you?" She looked up at me with a plea in her eyes. Damn, if I didn't want to kiss her at that moment to make all her doubts disappear. Instead, I let my hand roam on her back and into her hair, more tenderly than I had ever before.

"Because it wasn't up to me. I'd never force you to be with me, or anyone else for that matter. You were robbed of the choice before and I would never forgive myself if I'd take that choice away from you a second time."

"But I wasn't what I wanted. They told me to lie or they would have killed you. How did you know I wasn't telling the truth?"

"You're still wearing your wedding ring." Her mouth formed into an o. "If you really had gotten remarried, if you really had moved on and didn't want anything to do with me, I doubt you would have still been wearing *my ring*."

"You thought I got remarried?"

"I received wedding photos-"

"From my cousin's wedding?"

She seemed to play back the memory and come to the same conclusion. The woman in the photos had had similar features with only a few subtle differences. Perhaps in my delirium I had mistaken the bride as Katy.

"Explains the resemblance."

"What else?"

"A sonogram and a picture of a stomach round witch child."

"But you didn't believe that either?"

"No." I said, shaking my head. My fingertips traveled along the heaps and valleys of her side, leaving a trail of goosebumps in their wake. "I've touched, kissed and licked every inch of your gorgeous body. I've seen all of you. I know your body better than you know it yourself. I'd like to think I'd know exactly what you'd look like if you were pregnant."

As my fingers worked up her body, her breathing became more erratic. She bit her lip listening to my confession and let out an enamored moan.

"God, I love it when you say sappy shit like that."

She leaned in and kissed me. I had waited months to

taste her lips again. Every night I had dreamed of this exact moment where I had her back in my arms, kissing me just like this. I would have made it last longer, enjoyed the feel of her lips against mine if it weren't for that word. Breaking the kiss, I stared down at her.

"What?"

"I believe that is the first time you've said that."

She seemed to be just as shocked at her own words as I was. *Did she really say that?* Then her eyes softened. Her smile pulled at my heartstrings. Her hands resting on my shoulders, she kissed me again.

"Well, it's true. I've been in love with you ever since that day you got wounded in the ambush."

"You've known almost a year and didn't tell me?"

"I never got the chance. You sent me away." She hit my shoulder mockingly and warped her mouth into a sexy pout.

"Well it's a good thing I got you back then so you can tell me every day to make up for it."

"What about you?" The wild hammering against my ribs almost drowned out her question. It was as if my heart was about to burst right out of my chest. "Don't you love me too?"

"Katy."

Taking a deep breath, I leaned on my elbows, caging her between them. Despite her bruises, she looked devastatingly gorgeous beneath me, pressed down on the mattress. If she hadn't just gone through a traumatic event, I would have had her naked and close to an orgasm the moment she woke up.

Even now, as my cock was hard and aching to be inside her, I possessed enough willpower to not do just that. She deserved time to heal, time to work through her trauma.

Even if she would never want to be intimate ever again, I knew I'd be perfectly content with her happiness alone. She was my everything.

"There are no words strong enough to describe how I feel about you. You are mine, forever. I will be yours for as long as you live, and when your time comes, I will soon follow. You are the reason for my existence. There is no future without you in it."

"That may be the sweetest lie you've ever told."

"I've never lied to you, Katy. I love you, with every fiber of my being down to my bones."

"Say it again." A shiver ran through me, as I felt her lips on my neck. She peppered kisses on my exposed skin, pulling me even closer.

"I love you, Katy."

"Again." She moved up to my jaw and placed kisses there as well. She was making it very hard to be a gentleman as she wrapped her legs around my waist. Very, *hard.*

"I love you."

And then, I was a goner. Arms behind my neck, she pulled me on top of her, planting her lips firmly on mine. She took control of the kiss, working her fingers through my hair and tugging at the roots. Our tongues locked as we sunk deeper under the covers, entangled in each other's embrace.

Epilogue

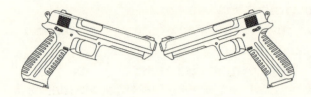

T hree weeks of therapy, two days of planning and one new tattoo later, I was finally feeling like myself again. Standing in front of the mirror, my eyes glazed over the healed ink adorning my abdomen. The snake heads of the medusa slithered across my chest and over my ribs in a twisting pattern. She was beautiful.

The mirror was a gorgeous antique piece that matched the rest of the new house. Since the penthouse had gotten completely destroyed during the attack, Jax had decided to relocate to a new district, populated by quaint and charming historical buildings. It was a cozy place just for the two of us. However, I was happy to see Louisa as part of the rotating staff since the house was smaller and didn't need to be staffed around the clock.

One of my favorite things about the house was the fenced in backyard. For now it was still under a heavy blanket of snow, but come spring I imagined myself spending a lot of time on the vine shrouded terrasse and planting the garden.

I felt like Jax and I were making up for lost time. We had resumed our date nights. For every night out on the town, wining, dinging and dancing, we balanced it with a night in, cuddling and watching movies. I had missed the domestic life with him.

He was still working hard recuperating all of the assets he had lost during our hardship. He had mended some of the broken relations and established new business deals, replacing the ones that Logan had sabotaged. According to Jax, Logan was responsible for everything that happened in the past year.

Getting dressed, I made sure to put on extra layers of fur to shield me from the cold. Jax was already waiting for me at the door when I skipped the last steps to meet him. He looked good enough to eat, dressed in all black and his hair pulled back with gel. He stole a kiss from my lips and escorted me to the car, before I got the chance to take it any further.

He had been a perfect gentleman during my recovery, giving me a lot of attention and raining me with affection. But he never took our makeout sessions below the waist. I appreciated his thoughtfulness during my recovery, but more than anything I wanted him to replace *that* memory with our own. In other words, I was getting really horny.

As he pulled the car out of the driveway, I made myself comfortable in the seat, angled my body towards him and slipped out of my boots. He was so focused on the road he didn't notice me lifting my legs over the gearshift till my feet were already in his lap. Giving me a soft glance, he placed a hand on my shin and rubbed it gently with his thumb. The warmth of his hand burned through my stockings.

"What are you doing, Katy?"

"Enjoying the ride, of course." I cooed.

Running my feet along the inside of his thigh, a low growl resonated in his throat. My toes curled over the bulge I knew would be growing in seconds. Teasing the length of his cock through his pants had him gripping the steering wheel harder and clenching his jaw.

"You're playing a dangerous game."

"I like danger, remember." I said, honey on my tongue and batting my eyelashes.

It took little to no effort to seduce my husband, but I enjoyed the chase nonetheless. Curling my toes around the tip of his cock earned me another growl. The grip he had on my leg tightened as a warning.

"Katy." The look in his eyes was both deadly and pained, filled with longing and lust.

"Eyes on the road."

"If you continue this-"

"You what? Gonna cum in your pants?" His breathing got heavier and I felt his cock twitch under my toes. "I know what I'm doing. That's exactly what's gonna happen."

Pressing the pad of my foot along his shaft, I mimicked the moves I knew how to make with my hands. His whole body shuddered, when I simultaneously rubbed my toes over the tip and the hard length of his cock. I could feel myself getting wet just from teasing him.

The car came to a halt at a stop sign and his hand left my shin long enough to unzip his pants. With the tip of my toes I freed his cock that was peeking from the waistband of his boxers. Squeezing his length between my feet, I made a jerky up and down motion till the head was slick with precum and soaking my stockings.

"God, Katy. You're killing me with this."

"Wouldn't it be a great way to die, though?"

All I got was a husky moan as he jerked his hips to match the movements of my feet, rubbing his piercing against my toes. With great struggle, he managed to turn the wheel and bring the car to another stop. He bit his fist, hiding the lewd face he was making when I wedged his cock between my toes, milking him.

"I'm so close."

"I know. Almost there." Meaning both his climax and our destination.

Pressing the pads of my feet together, I created a tight gap, adding more pressure and friction at the same time to the tip of his cock. I knew he was reaching the breaking point based on his ragged breathing. The car slowed down and pulled up to a familiar driveway. *Time to finish this.*

With one foot, I made circling motions over his head, while with the other I tickled his balls. His hips jutted up from the seat and with a final jerk of his cock, he spilled his cum all over my toes. Not even bothering to wipe my feet, I shoved them back into the boots and stepped out of the car.

Jax was still leaning against the headrest, reeling in from his climax when I wounded the car and strolled towards the mansion doors. I could see my breath in the air as the butler opened the door.

"Miss Valentina. Your father is in his study."

"Thank you, Mikhail. Is anyone around?"

"It seems everyone else is otherwise *occupied.*" He tapped the tip of his nose, gave me a knowing look and closed the door. I turned around in the foyer, shed my fur coat and gave it to his outstretched hands.

"My husband will follow me shortly. Would you mind getting the door for him and then wait for us in the car? This won't take long."

"Certainly, miss."

"That's all."

Not wasting any time, I climbed the grand staircase and headed straight to my father's office. The smell of him hit me before I even saw the door, cheap vodka and cigars. The hallway was barren and void of any clutter. A starking contrast to the lavish style I was used to seeing in this house.

"Priviet, Papa."

"Malyshka. What a pleasant surprise. I wasn't expecting you."

"As intended."

"Eh?"

Pulling out one of my throwing knives, I fung it at him with deadly precision I knew would cripple him. The blade dug straight into the soft tendon of his shoulder. The whites in his eyes bulged out as he let out a gut wrenching scream, cursing in our native tongue.

"What the fuck?!"

He reached for the hilt, spilling blood everywhere, as he pulled the blade out of the wound and tossed it at me. Dodging it with ease, I twirled another blade in my hand and prepared my next shot, taking aim.

"Now that I have your attention, let's have a little chat, shall we? Father to daughter." I said, motioning between us with my blade. The blood had begun to color his shirt red. Not his first cut, nor it would be his last.

"Surely we can have a civilized conversation without this-" He groaned. "-blood shed."

"See that's the thing, we can't."

"You're making a big mistake, malyshka."

He made a move to reach for the glock I knew he had hidden in his desk, the gun he had used many times on his enemies. With catlike reflexes, I flung the blade at his hand, pinning it to the wood. He bared his teeth at me, swallowing his groans of pain.

"You're a dead woman walking." With his uninjured hand, he reached for the silent alarm, while I twirled another blade in my fingers. I knew no one would answer his distress. "What have you done?"

"I should be asking 'what *you* have done', Papa. You see, Jax found some interesting details while looking into Logan's business dealings."

"What's that *kozyol* gotta do with this?"

"Well, turns out, you were a silent partner in almost all of his companies."

"That means nothing."

Ignoring him, I paced in the room, prowling like a beast looking at its prey. He made an attempt to remove the blade off his hand, but it was lodged deep in the wood.

Before he had the chance to rip his hand out, I swung the blade, digging a gaping laceration to his bicep and stabbing his elbow, pinning it to the desk as well. The roar he released pierced my ears.

"And since my marriage to him, however brief, I inherited every single one of those companies and their assets."

A pool had begun to form on the surface of the desk, filling my nostrils with the coppery stench of blood. My father looked stressed for the first time in his life. I thought he had finally realized I was going to kill him and there was nothing he could do to stop it. He was crucified.

"So? You got yourself a little enterprise and you think

you can go against me? I still got-"

"I'm not finished. You know what else he found?" Placing my knife horizontally over his finger, right below his knuckles, I looked him in the eyes and pushed the blade down with a satisfying crunch. I took great pleasure in his wails of agony. "Every contract you signed was made in mom's name. You're such a fucking coward you couldn't even sign you own name. She owns everything."

His breathing was ragged, short and shaken, he tried to mask by snarling at me again. Through gritted teeth he managed to keep the conversation going, barely. I enjoyed seeing him struggle.

"I'm sure I didn't raise an idiot." He said, while I shot back 'You didn't raise me at all', as he continued. "Yekaterina is dead."

"I'm aware. I was the one who found her body, remember. I was the little girl dressed in black at her funeral, remember."

With another blade, I stabbed him in the uninjured shoulder, then in the chest and ribs. With every hit, blood splattered all over me. I could feel the thick syrup run down my face. He tasted foul. I knew he didn't have much time left before he would bleed out.

"But you know what else I've seen too? Her will. Before she died, she wrote me a letter I found after her funeral."

"She did not-"

"Oh I'm sure you tried your best to throw away all her stuff to cover the fact that her last wish was to leave everything to me. For years I watched you. I watched, as you spent what was rightfully mine and I knew, you wouldn't give it up willingly. You were so comfortable surrounded by your men, acting like you were untouchable."

The glass he had been nursing was half empty. I grabbed it off the table and swallowed its contents, washing his taste out of my mouth before slamming the glass back on the table. *I hate warm vodka.*

"I knew I'd get you eventually, all I had to do was bide my time, take the abuse, go along with all your schemes, be the perfect little doll you thought you could manipulate and control."

With agility, I jumped on top of the desk, kicked him in the chest, dislodged him from the knives and sent him tumbling backwards. Choking on his own blood, he took his final word.

"Suka blyat-"

"Say hello to my mother." I stepped over him, readying my knife at his throat. "Dasvidaniya."

The knife sliced through the soft flesh, silencing him forever. Still burning with disgust, I hacked his chest, again and again, filling it with holes, bringing down the edge of the blade over and over again till I was completely drenched in his blood.

Shaking with adrenaline and relief, I barely noticed the arms that closed around me, pulling me away from the mangled corpse. Jax's soothing voice rumbled against my ear, as he pulled me in his embrace.

"That's enough. You did it. It's over."

He turned my face towards him by placing his fingers under my chin, and then he kissed me like I've never been kissed before. It was so intense, so full of lust mixed in with raw passion, I almost forgot where I was at.

"Stop. I'm all messy."

"I don't care. I'm going to kiss my beautiful wife who has been through hell and survived. You look absolutely gorgeous just like this, bathing in the blood of your enemy."

"Then I shall paint the whole world red."

Within minutes, I was out of the bloody clothes and in his lap, sitting in the back of the car. Mikhail had taken his spot in the driver's seat. With equal passion, I kissed Jax as the glow of the burning mansion shone through the back window. Rolling my hips, I felt his cock slip into my pussy making me moan in pleasure.

"God, I've missed you."

"There is no God here, only devils." He managed to say between kisses.

With hands on my hips, he guided my movements, urging me to begin moving faster, bouncing on his cock. Each thrust dug deeper, hitting me in the sensitive spot that drove me wild.

My hands glided through his hair, over his shoulders and down to his abs. I felt him shiver beneath me as my fingers traced over the old scar. He had covered it with characters from all the movies we had watched and there was still room to add more. It was my favorite part of him. *Well, second favorite.*

His mouth was on mine, working me into a frenzy, kissing every inch of me he could creach. When I felt his finger teasing the rim of my ass, I was lost and began to ride him faster, rocking my hips at a vigorous pace. His other hand moved to my pussy, putting pressure on my already sensitive clit.

While the night sky was lit up with fireworks, the rest of the world seemed to fade away as we took each other to the edge of oblivion.

The end